1118

FIC
LAN

SLOW BULLET

SLOW BULLET

JOHN L. LANSDALE

BookVoice Publishing 2017

Slow Bullet Copyright © 2017
by John L. Lansdale
All rights reserved.

Cover art Copyright © 2014
by Jarred Murry
All rights reserved.

Interior design Copyright © 2017
by BookVoice Publishing
All rights reserved.

ISBN
978-0-9990361-1-2

BookVoice Publishing
PO Box 1528
Chandler, TX 75758
www.bookvoicepublishing.com

Novels by John L. Lansdale

Slow Bullet
Zombie Gold
Horse of a Different Color
Shadows West (with Joe R. Lansdale)
Hell's Bounty (with Joe R. Lansdale)

Coming Soon

Long Walk Home
The Last Good Day
Broken Moon
When the Night Bird Sings (Novella)
Shadow Warrior (Graphic Novel)
Justin Case (Graphic Novel)

Follow the author online at
www.bookvoicepublishing.com
www.facebook.com/johnllansdale
www.twitter.com/johnllansdale
www.goodreads.com/johnllansdale

For
Meleaha
1 & 2

"The older I get the younger everyone else locks."
Rick Daily

"For everything gained something is lost."
Anonymous

Part 1
Wrong Hand

1

The sound of Huey Helicopters in the distance meant the beginning. The ironic part was I never felt more alive than when I faced death. I checked my ammo and loaded a full magazine into my M-16. The barrel was cold and damp from a long night of silence. A slow wind brought a lingering smell of garlic that told me Charlie had arrived.

The rising sun silhouetted the hoard of gunships in the morning sky as they fired rockets at enemy positions. The screams of death fueled my basic instincts of survival and a feeling of exhilaration flooded my mind. Better him than me. I heard the dreaded sound of an incoming mortar round that exploded a few feet from me. The concussion of the blast knocked me down. I checked all my body parts. I didn't see any blood, but my ears wouldn't stop ringing. I put my hands over my ears and the ringing still wouldn't stop.

My eyes popped open. I was in bed, the phone ringing. My pulse was racing, my brain speeding through a forty-year corridor from past to present. I switched on a lamp and fumbled on the table for my cell phone. I knocked an open bottle of Jack Daniels off the table and spilled most of it on the floor. I took a deep breath and said, "Hello."

"Colonel, it's Bobby Spicier. Sorry to wake you so early."

"Not a problem. I wasn't sleeping good anyway. How's my godson?"

"I have bad news…my mom and dad are dead," he said, his voice cracking.

I was wide awake now. "What happened, a car wreck?"

"No. The D.C. police called about 1:30 this morning. A neighbor found them sometime after 10 last night. Said it looked like dad shot mom then turned the gun on himself. That's crazy, he would never do that."

My mind instantly traveled back in time. My "A-Team" was dropped into a firefight by helicopter on a bloody hill in Vietnam. I was hit, blood gushing from my leg, Charlie closing in for the kill when Captain Robert Spicier charged up the hill, guns blazing. He lifted me on his back and outran Charlie to our lines, firing an M-16 over his shoulder to slow them down. He never got a scratch.

"Colonel, you still there?"

"Yes, Bobby, I'm here. I was thinking about your dad. Did they find a note?"

"Nothing, there was nothing. You think it had anything to do with the company?"

"Could be. Anything's possible when you work for the CIA. How's your sister taking this?"

"Don't know, I haven't been able to locate her. She may have seen it on the news. Last I heard she had joined the Army and was in Iraq. She never bothered to tell us what unit

14

she was in. She hurt mom and dad bad. They had a daughter in the war and didn't know where. That boyfriend of hers was over there. I think that's why she joined. I haven't talked to her in over a year."

"That's too bad. I'll see if I can find her."

"Thanks, Colonel. Can you come to Washington and help me sort this out?"

"I'll see when I can get a flight."

"I don't want to stay at the house," he said. "I'll rent us a motel room. Call my cell when you get there."

"See you in Washington," I said.

I got up and walked stiff-legged to the bathroom. The natural effects of a man soon to be eligible for Social Security made it harder to get everything working like it used to. I looked in the mirror and saw what was left of Clark McKay, a once-proud man.

I looked like shit. I needed a haircut and had a four-day-old beard. My eyes looked like a lightning storm and my hands were shaking.

I got dressed, cleaned up the best I could, packed a bag and booked a flight to Washington. I wasn't the man I used to be, or even the one I pretended to be, but I owed it to myself as well as Robert to try to find the courage to make one last run. I knew he would do it for me.

I was good at killing people, finding a killer was a different story. It might be more than I could handle.

I picked up the whiskey bottle, shook it turned it up and drank the last drop. I realized what I was doing and threw it against the wall, busting it into a thousand pieces. I stared at the man in the mirror, looking for a sign of the old me but didn't see one. I wiped a tear from my eyes

This was going to be hard.

2

The flight from Dallas to Washington lasted through two double shots of Jack Daniels, a bag of peanuts, a trip to the bathroom, a short snooze and 20 pages of People Magazine, give or take a page or two.

I got my bag, picked up my rental car, bought a fifth of Jack and found the motel with some help from a grizzled old man walking his dog. I pulled into a parking space next to Robert's Lincoln Town Car. For a moment, I could see him sitting behind the wheel smiling at me.

Bobby appeared at the motel door. "Thanks for coming, Colonel," he said.

"I'm so very sorry, Bobby. I know how it feels to lose your family."

"I know you do," he said. "I picked up dad's car. I'm having mom and dad transferred from the morgue to a funeral home as soon as they're ready. No word from Pepper yet."

"Maybe we will hear from her before the funeral," I said. He nodded and carried my bag into the motel room.

"I went to the house," he said. "I didn't get to go in. The police were there. I did get the neighbors to take care of Scooter and meet the lead detective. Here's his card."

He handed me the card and I couldn't help grinning when I saw the name. It was an oxymoron. Maybe Lieutenant Sonny Goodnight was still there. We needed to talk. I dialed the number and a man with a gravelly voice like a bullfrog and a New England accent answered.

"Desk Sergeant Baldona, how can I help you?" he said.

"Lieutenant Goodnight, please."

"He's gone for the day. Can I help?"

"No, I need to talk to the Lieutenant. Would you leave a message for him that Bobby Spicier and Clark McKay will be in to see him tomorrow, it's about the Spicier case."

"He may not have time to see you."

"I'll take my chances," I said and hung up.

Bobby and I talked about old times before forcing ourselves to talk about the funeral. Since he couldn't get in touch with his sister, he and his aunt Sara decided to bury them in their hometown of Hustly, South Carolina. Listening to him talk was like being with Robert 30 years ago. He had the same good looks as his dad, smile and voice, even the little nostril flare when he took a deep breath. But his personality was more like his mother's, quiet and unassuming.

On the other hand, his sister had that same fire in the belly as her dad and marched to her own drum. She almost didn't graduate from law school because she refused to be on the same stage as the commencement speaker who she neither liked nor respected.

I wondered how she was taking this. She had to know by now. I hoped she didn't do anything foolish.

3

The morning came quick, and we arrived at the police station a little after 9 A.M. There was a no parking zone in front of the station so I parked in a paid parking lot across the street.

The police station was a two-story, red brick building with bar-covered windows.

We approached a desk that had an information sign dangling on a chain from the ceiling. Behind the desk on the wall was a picture of the President. A foul perspiration odor danced across the room – too many people too often.

A small pudgy man with receding hair, beady eyes, and a too-tight uniform with sergeant stripes looked up from the desk, saw us and stood up. He rested his right elbow on the butt of an automatic strapped to his waist and stuck the thumb of his other hand in his gun belt.

"Can I help you gentleman?" he asked. It was the bullfrog.

"We're here to see Lieutenant Goodnight. It's about the Spicier case," I said.

"I recognize that voice," he said. "You're the guy I talked to yesterday. You're not from around here."

"Nope," I said.

"Don't know if I should bother the Lieutenant this early, he has a lot of reports to look over."

"Sergeant, we've come a long way. We need to see him."

He hesitated for a moment to consider, pointed to a hallway. "Last door on the left."

I knocked on a door with 'Lt. Goodnight' painted on it. A voice from the other side said, "Come in."

I opened the door and a tall thin man in a dark blue suit with a neatly-trimmed black mustache and horn-rimmed glasses stood up and motioned for us to come in. He had a dimpled chin and needed a sharper razor. His thick black hair parted in the middle made him look like one of those untouchable characters from the gangster movies. He was placing a telephone back in its cradle. A call from the sergeant no doubt.

An In and Out basket was overflowing with papers. Several folders were stacked on the desk. The folder on top had Spicier written on it. An 8x10 picture of a pretty dark-haired woman with two small boys in a silver picture frame sat on the other side of the desk. A college diploma and two commendations for valor hung on the wall behind him.

"Lieutenant Goodnight, I'm Clark McKay and this is Bobby Spicier, Robert's son."

"Yes, Bobby and I met yesterday. He mentioned you." We shook hands.

"Have a seat," he said.

We sat down and Lieutenant Goodnight expressed his sympathy for Bobby's loss of his parents and asked my relationship to the deceased. I explained I was a longtime friend and Bobby was my godson. He didn't say anything but I could tell he was a bit surprised.

"Bobby referred to you as Colonel," Goodnight said. "That honorary or military?"

"Military. Army," I said.

Goodnight nodded and looked at the folder. "You never know what people will do," he said, clasping his hands together on the desk in front of him, his thumbs making circular motions as he spoke.

"That's why we're here, Lieutenant," I said.

Bobby wrinkled his brow and leaned forward, his eyes fixed on Goodnight in a cold stare. "The first thing I want to know, Lieutenant, is why you think my dad could do such a thing? I can't imagine that possibility."

"I'm sorry, Bobby. There may be things that you don't know. Secrets that a father didn't want his son to know. I've learned to never assume anything. The facts we have indicate your dad shot your mother, then himself. We've finished the preliminary report. Normally we don't show family members our reports, however in this case there seems to be reason for an exception. I can show you the report if you think you can handle it. It's very graphic. It may be something you don't want to see."

"What do you think, Bobby?" I asked.

Little beads of sweat popped out on his forehead. He took a handkerchief out of his pocket and wiped his forehead, sighed and placed the handkerchief back in his pocket.

"Yeah...I have to know," he said, nodding his head up and down.

"Show us," I said, leaning closer to the desk.

He picked up the folder and began sorting pictures and papers.

"There was no forced entry," he said. "Nothing to indicate anyone else had been in the house. No unknown fingerprints. Nothing appeared to be missing. Bobby, you can verify the contents later if you will."

Bobby nodded.

"The only ones who saw or heard anything live next door. A Mr. and Mrs. Morgan. They heard the Spiciers' dog barking, went to check, saw them through a window and called 911. The only thing out of the ordinary was a faint odor that we have not identified. The lab boys are working on that. We believe Mr. Spicier shot his wife in the head, then himself. You can see from these pictures that the bullet entered the left temple just above the ear of Mrs. Spicier and exited on the other side of the head."

A colored 8x10 showed a small hole in her left temple with a trickle of blood running down the side of her head. Another picture showed a hole the size of a baseball where the bullet came out, with brain matter and blood splattered on her head, neck and the shoulders of her bright emerald green house coat.

Bobby's eyes began to water. He jumped up and ran from the room to the bathroom. I followed him. He was vomiting in the commode. When there was nothing left he wiped his mouth with toilet paper.

"My god, how could anyone do such a thing. She never hurt a fly. This is something I wasn't prepared for. I don't think I can go back in there." He dabbed at the tears on his face with more toilet paper.

"Why don't you wash your face and wait for me up front," I said. "I'll see what else he has and we'll get out of here."

"Yeah. I'll do that." He wiped more tears. "Sorry, Colonel."

"Hey, it's okay. I'm barely hanging on myself." We walked out of the bathroom. I returned to Goodnight's office and Bobby took a seat by the front door.

"He okay?" Goodnight asked. "I warned you."

"Yeah he'll be alright."

He paused for a few seconds to give me time to change my mind, and then continued. He laid more pictures on the desk showing the wounds and the death faces of Elle and Robert. Robert was wearing a blue sweat shirt and jeans with the same bullet effects as Elle. They both had their eyes closed. That in its self seemed unusual. Something about dying from the shock of a bullet left most people with an open eyed fixed stare. Not always, but most of the time. Goodnight waited for me to finish my examination of the pictures and continued.

"Mr. Spicier's fingerprints were the only ones on the .45 automatic that inflected the wounds," he said. "There was residue on his left hand. As an old friend, I am sure you know Mr. Spicier was left-handed."

"None on the right hand?"

"No, why?"

"Then he didn't do it. He was left handed but he shot with his right hand."

Goodnight laid the folder down, clasped his hands and began the circular motion with his thumbs again.

"The autopsies are not complete but we know for sure they were shot while sitting because of the lack of blood flow in the lower extremities of the bodies. We believe Mr. Spicier did it. They were sitting in the chairs watching TV. The TV was still on. Mr. Spicier shot Mrs. Spicier, who was sitting to his right, in the left temple with his left hand by turning in the chair to his right and raising the gun to her head with his left hand. Then he placed the gun to his left temple and fired. I'm sorry, but that's what happened."

With that remark, he closed the folder. That was supposed to be my cue to leave. I sat staring at the closed folder thinking it sounded so logical, yet knowing that's not what happened.

"Lieutenant, I have to agree with Bobby. This whole thing just doesn't ring true. I knew the man for over 40 years. He was one of the most confident, self-assured individuals I have ever known. He wouldn't doubt himself enough to pull the trigger on his life or anyone else's. He loved life and his wife too much to do that. We were both left-handed, but fired weapons right-handed, not left-handed. You form habits. I don't think he would have reverted to something foreign to him. His military file will verify that. It would have been very difficult to shoot himself in the left temple with his right hand, which is the hand he would have fired the weapon with. That's how I know he didn't do it."

"That's pure speculation. You can't change the facts, Mr. McKay."

"That's where you're wrong," I said.

He removed his glasses, ran a Kleenex hard over them, put them back on and leaned back in his chair.

"Mr. McKay, I don't make this stuff up. These are facts. The residue was on his left hand. None on the right as I told you before." He looked at the folder and tapped it with his index finger. "Facts," he said. "Facts, not hearsay."

"Goodnight, whoever killed Robert and Elle made the same mistake you're making. They thought they did their research and placed the gun in his left hand, but that was wrong. They were murdered and I'm going to prove it."

His jaw tightened, his eyes blinked. I had pissed him off big-time. He pushed the folder aside and we both stood up watching each other like two boxers waiting for the other one to throw the next punch.

"You're over your head, McKay. Start meddling in this case and I will get a restraining order. You and Bobby take care of burying the Spiciers and let me do my job. I know Mr. Spicier was a war hero and a good black man. I am sorry this happened. I—"

"What do you mean a good black man?" I interjected. "If it were me, would you say I was a good white man? I don't think so. How about a good man period." I clenched my fist then realized what I was doing and relaxed my hands.

"It was just a figure of speech," he said. "I didn't mean any harm. This is beginning to get out of hand. Being belligerent won't bring your friend back, McKay. I suggest you leave now and remember what I told you. Stay out of this."

"Gladly, but you should know - I got a good memory, it's just short."

Goodnight took a deep breath, dropped his head slightly and looked over his glasses. "Well, maybe you better take a memory course, McKay, because I meant what I said."

"So did I," I said. "So did I. Is it okay for us to go in the house?"

"As long as you don't remove anything without clearing it with me," Goodnight said. He reached in his desk drawer and took out two pair of nylon gloves. "Slip these on when you go in. It will make it easier for the lab boys. We should be through with the investigation in another day or two."

"Okay," I said and took the gloves from him.

After a brief stare down, I walked away.

Bobby was sitting on a bench with two women. They looked like prostitutes from the way they were dressed. Bobby politely said goodbye to the smiling ladies and joined me. We pushed open the double doors and walked across the street to Robert's Lincoln.

"Learn anything that will help us figure this out, Colonel?"

"Your dad didn't kill your mother and he didn't shoot himself."

"I know that, but how are we going to convince anyone else?"

"We're going to need help to make the police listen to us. That detective sure as hell isn't going to listen to me. I have a friend in the FBI, I'll call him. There's something wrong with all of this. Something out of place, a piece missing. Robert was a good agent. It's odd that someone could get that close without a fight."

"That's what I was thinking," Bobby said.

"Let's take a look in the house if you're up to it. Maybe we'll find something the police overlooked."

"I'm okay. That was just a horrible shock."

"Yeah I know. I didn't handle it very well either. I definitely got off on the wrong foot with Goodnight.

4

On the way to the house I searched my mind for a reason anyone would want to kill Robert and Elle. It had to be something to do with Robert's work. But what? None of it made sense. Robert hadn't worked in the field in two years. His secret work was behind him. He was riding a desk, working on dead files for storage. We had talked about it less than two weeks ago. He told me how boring it was and that he was retiring soon. As for Elle, she must have been in the wrong place at the wrong time.

The house was a Chicago brick in a quiet, neat neighborhood between D.C. and Arlington, Virginia. Robert and Elle had lived there for the last twenty years. Most of the people in the area worked for the government in one capacity or another.

We slipped on the gloves and went in. Goodnight was right about one thing, nothing seemed disturbed except for the blood stains on and around the chairs and the TV. There was a hint of an unfamiliar odor that we didn't recognize. Must likely the smell Goodnight was referring to. Nothing else was different. That was it. You expected Robert and Elle to walk in any moment and discover it was all a bad joke.

Bobby found some insurance papers and keepsakes he wanted and called Goodnight for approval to remove them. We decided to come back another day. We locked the house and got in the car.

"Someone has gone to a lot of trouble to keep us from knowing what really happened to your mom and dad, Bobby. If we're not careful we may be next."

"Dad has guns in the house. Maybe we should get us a gun."

"Don't think so. We don't want to kill anyone, at least not yet."

I was backing the car out of the drive when an old man appeared on the lawn. The few strands of white hair left on his head were blowing back and forth. His face was sprinkled with age spots. He had a hearing aid in his ear, glasses hanging around his neck on a chain and a wobble in his legs like a scarecrow in a high wind.

"Wait," Bobby said. "That's Mr. Morgan, Dad's next-door neighbor. I forgot, I need to thank him for taking care of Scooter."

I stopped the car and cut the engine. We got out and walked across the lawn to the old man.

"This is Mr. Morgan," Bobby said. "Mr. Morgan and his wife have been Dad and Mom's neighbors for twenty years. I just realized you haven't met. Mr. Morgan, this is my godfather, Colonel Clark McKay."

As we shook hands I prepared myself to catch the old man if necessary. "Mr. Morgan, would you mind if I asked you a question or two?"

"Fire away sonny, but make it quick, I have to get off my feet. I just wanted to see how Bobby was doing. I'm real sorry about Robert and Elle."

"I'm okay, sir, thanks," Bobby said.

"Mr. Morgan what happened?" I said.

"Me and Maggie were getting ready for bed. We heard a noise. I still had my hearing aids in so I heard it pretty good. It was like two pieces of metal rubbing together, loud, told the police, but don't think they believed me. I didn't see anything, but I did hear the noise"

"Do you know if anyone else heard it?" I asked.

"Didn't see anyone else come out of any of the houses. Police didn't say anyone else did. May have been just me and Maggie."

"You think it was a gun shot?"

"No, nothing like a gunshot. It was like when someone rubs their fingernails on a blackboard; ear piecing, goes all through you. That was it until the dog started barking about 30 minutes later. He was carrying on like crazy. He kept on so I told Maggie to go see why he was barking. That's when she saw Elle through the window and called 911. A terrible thing it was. Scooter was still barking when the ambulance got there. Maggie brought him to the house but he didn't calm down for an hour after that. Animals know when something's wrong, you know. Little fellow was scared to death."

"You didn't hear gun shots?" I asked again.

"Nope, we had the TV going at the time. I had turned it off right before we heard that strange sound." The old man shifted his weight from one leg to the other. "Pardon me while I find a backstop. My ass moves out from under my feet sometime."

"You're sure you heard the metal rubbing sound before the dog started barking?"

"I'm sure. I told that Goodnight fellow about it. Wasn't just me, my wife heard it too."

"Maybe that's what he was responding to," I said. "You remember what time you heard the sound?"

"Not for sure. Maybe around ten o'clock, a little before. I don't know what it was, don't hear too good anymore, but I heard that."

"You didn't hear the metal sound earlier? Just that once, around 10?"

"Nope," he said. "I got to go in now, my old legs are about gone."

I saw a woman looking out the window, assumed it was Maggie and waved. She moved away and didn't wave back.

"Bobby, I'm sorry about your mom and dad," the old man said. "Pass my sympathies on to Pepper. They were good people. Such a shame. You can pick up the dog when you're ready. Maggie will take good care of him."

"Thanks Mr. Morgan," Bobby said. "Your wife has my phone number in case you need me. I've got to get a place where they let me keep pets before I can pick him up."

"Oh, I almost forgot," the old man said. "Two men came by yesterday asking questions about you and the Colonel. Wanted to know if you had been to the house and where you were staying. One was a big fellow, the other one kind of skinny. The big fellow said he used to work with Robert, had hands like a gorilla. When they headed for their car I overheard him say, 'I'll send my boys after them.'"

"You're sure that's what he said?"

"Yep, that's what he said. Sounded like a threat to me."

"Thank you," I said.

"Got to go," he said, shrugged his shoulders, turned and began taking baby steps toward his house.

We climbed back in the Lincoln and took off.

"You think he's telling the truth Bobby?" I asked.

"Yes, he's a retired state department man. He may not have it right but I think that's what he thought he heard." Bobby said.

"I have a friend in the FBI, I'll give him a call. We need some help," I said.

5

When we got back to the motel I poured a glass of Jack and called my FBI friend Sam Tutt. The three of us served together in Nam. He said he would meet me the next day at noon at the Vietnam Memorial. Considering the circumstances that seemed appropriate.

The next morning, Bobby left around 9:30 to set up transportation for his mom and dad to Hustly, SC and spend some time at the funeral home.

I got up, filled my coffee cup with Jack, popped some Tylenol to ease some scar tissue, watched TV and read the morning paper. A suicide bombing in Afghanistan killed 16 civilians and two American soldiers. It was getting worse and everything indicated a failed plan.

On the way to the memorial I stopped at a sporting goods store and bought some insurance in the form of a 34-ounce Mickey Mantle Louisville Slugger, in case someone had any physical objections to me being here. To my surprise, I found a lone Cowboys football jacket that fit on a back shelf away from the neatly displayed Redskins jackets up front. I put the jacket on and laid the bat in the back seat.

Sam was standing in front of the memorial wearing the typical FBI uniform. A dark suit, white shirt, black tie, black shoes, overcoat, sunglasses and a Marlboro filter king clenched between his teeth. Sam was about 5'10" with close-cut thin gray hair, a weathered face with crow's feet extending out from under his sunshades. He was too thin from smoking too many cigarettes. He always had fingernail clippers with him and constantly clipped his nails out of nervous habit. I didn't know much about Sam's personal life, except he had an ex-wife. He would always change the subject. I was going to check his records but felt guilty and never did.

A gust of cold wind hit my face. I turned the collar up on my new Cowboys jacket, put my back to the wind and wished I was back in Texas.

Sam saw me and walked over and reached out to shake hands.

"How are you Sam?" I said as we shook hands.

"What's it been, five years?" he asked.

"Yes. As a matter of fact it has been five years, three months and twenty eight days since I buried Mary and Cooper."

"Sorry, Clark. I didn't mean to bring up old pain."

"It's alright. It doesn't take much to trigger it. You been waiting long?"

"No, I came a little early to look at the wall." He took a long drag on a short cigarette, took it out of his mouth, rubbed the fire out with his fingers, shredded the butt and dropped it in his pocket.

"Still field-stripping cigarettes," I said.

"Yep, old habits die hard," he said, paused and gestured toward the shrine. "There's a lot of names on that wall we know, Clark. Why them and not us?"

"I've asked myself that question a thousand times, Sam. It's like the day Mary and Cooper were killed in the car wreck. Cooper was coming home from college for spring break. I was running late and asked Mary to pick him up at the airport instead of me. I'll never forgive myself. Maybe I should have been one of those guys on the wall."

"It wasn't your fault, Clark. Just like it wasn't our fault we survived the war and they didn't."

"Well, we were young and naive Sam. Thought we were Supermen. In some ways we were. We came home; over 50,000 didn't. Life doesn't make a whole lot of sense sometimes."

"That's for sure. Like now," he said.

"How did you hear about Robert and Elle, Sam?"

"I saw something on TV, then confirmed it with the police."

"They said Robert shot Elle and himself with his left hand, Sam .He shot right handed. We were both left-handed but shot right-handed. We couldn't close our right eye. You remember that don't you?"

Sam gave me a deadpan look. "Yeah, now I remember. Why didn't I remember that?"

"You're getting old like me."

"What were you saying?"

"See."

"You got me," he said and laughed.

Sam pulled out his nail clippers and chopped off a small piece of nail from his right index finger, surveyed the others, placed the nail clippers back in his pocket and buttoned the top button on his overcoat.

"I'm freezing my ass off, Sam. Tell me what we need to do so we can get out of this weather."

"This is not your game, Clark. Leave it to the professionals before something bad happens to you."

"You know I can't do that."

"Well it's your funeral as they say, but in this case that could really happen. If I was you, I would get rid of that damn jacket; it's like a bullseye."

"Can't do that, Sam, the Cowboys would never forgive me."

Sam chuckled, pulled out another cigarette and lit it.

"You know those things are killing you," I said.

"I'll be long dead from other causes before the cigarettes get me. Hell, I would smoke them in my sleep if someone would hold them. We all have our demons. I'm sure you would agree."

"Can't argue with that," I said. "I climbed into a bottle five years ago and can't get out."

"Let me find out who's doing what and I'll get back to you as soon as I can," he said. "Wish you would take my advice and go home after the funeral."

"Thanks, but no thanks."

"You're making a mistake, Clark."

"We'll see. Let me know if you find out anything. I need all the help I can get."

"More than you realize," he said.

"See ya, Sam."

"I'll be in touch," he said.

We shook hands and I headed to my car.

I stopped for a burger, did some shopping off the rack for a plain leather jacket, suit, shirt and tie for the funeral and headed back to the motel, thinking about what might have happened to Robert and Elle.

6

I opened the motel door and saw a note on a pillow and picked it up. It read:

MCKAY,
IF YOU WANT TO KNOW WHO KILLED THE SFICIERS
COME TO 21343 RICER ROAD DRIVE AT SIX TODAY.
COME ALONE.

It was 5:40 now. I stopped a UPS guy that was delivering packages to the motel. "That's how you get there,' he said. "but I don't think you want to go there, mister."

I kept repeating the directions to myself as I drove and called Bobby four times and was told his phone was not in service. Where the hell was he? He needed to know where I was going in case I didn't come back. I left a message. Maybe they have Bobby. All kinds of possibilities ran through my mind. Goodnight may be right. I was in over my head.

The street was a rundown old business district with dilapidated buildings. Grass was growing through the cement cracks in the parking lots. For five blocks a wooded area covered one side of the street, old buildings on the other side. A setting sun behind the buildings threw shadows across the street, creating distorted monster-looking figures against the trees. A dirt road had been cut into the underbrush by people discarding old appliances and trash. Used syringes dotted both sides of the street. A sickening smell of waste and decay filled my nostrils and I was back in the war for a moment.

Two cars parked on the dirt road sped away as I approached.

A partly torn down chain link fence with the numbers 21343 on it stood in front of a large rusted metal building, some of the roof had blown off and was scattered around the parking lot. The big rollup loading doors had fallen off and I could see patches of fading sun light in the crumbling building.

I had a lump in my throat big as a baseball wondering what I had gotten myself into. I didn't know who or what I would find and wasn't sure I wanted to. I could have used some whiskey but I didn't bring it. This was where my military training was supposed to kick in. "To overcome fear take action."

I drove through the open fence, pulled up in front of the building and cut the engine. Shadows of something moving in the building in front of me caught my eye. As the images became clearer I saw an old brown Cadillac with a dented front fender coming toward me. My first thought was to haul ass. I reached in the floorboard of the backseat, wrapped my fingers around the bat handle, slid across the seat, opened the passenger door and got out on the opposite side from the Cadillac.

I placed the slugger against the side of the car, leaned over the top, both hands showing, watching the car approach. It looked like an ambush but I had to find out. The Cadillac stopped about ten yards from me and two men got out. One was a muscled-up big man with a serious case of the ugly. He had beard stubble over a ruddy complexion and a roman nose like a bad road curve. He wore faded jeans and a short sleeve blue shirt. A red devil's head was tattooed on his upper left arm with the words 'HOT STUFF' above the head with flames bellowing out of it. His bulging muscles stretched the seams of his shirt sleeves. It was too cold to be wearing a short sleeve shirt. A real dumb ass I thought.

The other one had a shaved head and was smaller and thinner, with a pearl earring in his right ear and a smooth baby face. He was wearing a green t-shirt with 'HARDCORE' across the front, a white sequined wind breaker and white jeans stuffed into white patent leather boots with tousles. If he wasn't gay he could fool a lot of people.

"Where's your nigger?" Rudface said, taking quick looks in different directions as they moved closer to the driver's side of my car.

"How do you know Bobby?" I asked.

"We have our ways," Mr. Sparkle said.

"Actually, Bobby prefers just Bobby. If race has to come into play, African-American or black is good. Sometime even colored is okay from someone he likes. For you two, 'saint' would piss him off. I'll just hurt you. He would put you six feet under."

"Oh yeah? You're full of shit, old man. Bring it on," Mr. Sparkle said.

"I wondered if you would be stupid enough to believe that note," Rudface said. "Maybe the nigger is smarter than you. He had the good sense not to show up." Rudface looked at Mr. Sparkle. Mr. Sparkle nodded his approval and they began to separate.

I reached down and placed my hand on the slugger. "What do you morons want?"

"You," Rudface said. "You ask too many questions."

"Who sent you?" I asked.

"That's out little secret," Mr. Sparkle said. "You're going down. This is your last giddy-up, cowboy."

"I wouldn't count on that," I said.

Rudface made a wave of his head and Mr. Sparkle began to move to the front of the car. Rudface stepped backwards until he was standing by the back wheel. They were going to come at me from both directions. I didn't see a gun. They must think they didn't need one. I hoped they were wrong. They hadn't seen the bat leaning against my leg.

Mr. Sparkle charged from the front of the car. I dropped my hands and wrapped them around the bat handle, turned and swung the bat from the ground up with my best homerun swing and caught him square between the legs. His pants made a swishing sound and stuck in his crotch. He fell to his knees, his mouth opening and closing like it was on hinges, nothing coming out. His eyes were bouncing around like cherries in a slot machine. He let out a monstrous moan, grabbed where his balls used to be, and fell facedown on the ground. He drew his legs up until his knees were touching his chest, his mouth open. He exhaled and went limp.

Rudface was on me now. I swung the bat to hit anything I could before he got a hold of me. A bull whip sound echoed across the dilapidated parking lot. He backed off, yelling, "You broke my arm, you bastard!"

"I hope so."

He was trying to get his other hand in his pocket. I came down on it with the bat as hard as I could. A screeching noise came out of his mouth like an eighteen wheeler coming to a sudden stop. He held his hand up with his other hand, looking at it. His fingers bent in different directions like branches on a dead tree limb.

He staggered toward me, struggling to stay on his feet. I slammed the bat square on his kneecap. He stopped in place and fell to the ground on his good leg, holding the damaged one off the ground like a dog pissing, his eyes watering. "Damn that hurt," he said, clenched his teeth and crashed to the ground with a thud and didn't move.

I fished a .22 automatic and his car keys out of one pants pocket and threw them as far as I could. He had a book of matches with Twisted Lizard Gentleman's Club printed on the cover in his other pocket.

I searched Mr. Sparkle. He hadn't moved since he went down. He had on too much cologne, 45 cents and a condom in his pockets. He wouldn't be needing the condom, at least not for a while.

Each man had several hundred dollars in their wallets, a driver's license, with no papers or phone numbers.

Mr. Sparkle's real name was Reggie Sloan. Rudface's was Diego Sanfini. I liked the names I gave them better.

I dropped their wallets and money on the ground beside them and drove back to civilization.

I checked my cell phone and discovered there was a call from a number I didn't recognize. I was still coming down from my fiasco with Rudface and Mr. Sparkle and it took me a minute or two for the light to come on. I dialed the number and the funeral home answered. Sure enough, that's where Bobby was. "Bobby, I've been worried sick about you."

"I've been here. I turned my phone off. They don't want cell phones ringing."

"Right, I should have known that. I'm on my way there."

I thought about my parents as I drove to the funeral home. They had been dead for many years but I missed them every day. The memories of my wife and only son were always on my mind, now here I was again. It was like being on a never-ending treadmill.

Bobby was sitting by the caskets when I walked in. It was going to be a long night.

7

The next morning Bobby and I checked out of the motel early, turned in my rental and drove to Hustly, South Carolina in Robert's Lincoln. I decided not to tell Bobby about the two thugs.

The only businesses open in Hustly was a burger place that used to be a Dairy Queen, a small medical clinic, a combination mercantile, grocery store and pharmacy, one of four pump service stations, a rusted-tir. feed store and a small post office with Old Glory waving outside.

Three old black men wearing overalls sat at a picnic table beside the post office pushing dominoes around, greeting everyone who passed.

A Greyhound bus with Columbia on the front pulled up to the feed store and two young black women with cardboard suitcases got on. The town's population got smaller every year. At the end of the street I saw a rusted movie marquee sign hanging over a crumbling theater with the admission prices still on the marquee. 'ADULTS 50 CENTS, CHILDREN 25 CENTS' the sign read.

Hustly had fallen on hard times years ago when the U.S. Government closed down the insulation plant for failure to meet environmental standards.

Robert's dad was one of the workers who lost their job. George Spicier developed lung cancer from working in the plant and died when Robert was twelve. He lost his mother two years later to pneumonia.

Sara turned the big house into a bed and breakfast to survive, and Robert left Hustly at eighteen and worked his way through a nearby black college and a commission as a second Lieutenant in the U.S. Army. He told me his life story every time he had too much to drink. He vowed he would never go back. I hoped he didn't know.

I parked in front and went in. Two caskets were in a large sitting room surrounded by yellow roses. Fifteen or twenty early-American-styled chairs were lined up against the walls for guest. A huge gold-framed mirror hung over a stone fireplace reflecting the rosewood caskets. A winding staircase ran to an upstairs hall. The elegance of the old house made it the perfect place to say goodbye to Robert and Elle. Both caskets were open for viewing.

A woman with gray hair neatly rolled into a bun, a little overweight, wearing a stylish black dress saw us come in and walked over to me and Bobby. She had a look in her eyes that told you she knew hard times intimately.

"Clark ?" she said with a tired smile. "I'm glad you could make it."

"Thanks, Sara, I'm so sorry. Robert and Elle were like family."

"They both felt the same about you." She turned her attention to Bobby and gave him a big hug. "Bobby, baby, why don't you go sit down and rest a while before the funeral."

"I'm okay, Aunt Sara. I'll just stay with the Colonel."

"Suit yourself, baby. Have you heard anything from Amanda?"

"No," Bobby said. "I guess she's not coming. You know Pepper, she's as unpredictable as the wind."

"It's been in the papers and on TV. Surely she knows," Sara said.

"I'll find her, Sara. I promise," I said.

She shook her head, wiped fresh tears away and excused herself to greet guests.

I met Elle's mother, Ruby, for the first time. You could tell she was a looker in her youth. Big brown eyes, cream-smooth complexion, and high cheek bones. She looked younger than I knew she had to be. I wasn't sure if she was black or white. I didn't ask. Elle and Pepper had that same beauty

In an ironic twist, Elle's dad died a few years after George Spicier from the same kind of cancer and Ruby went back to Boston to live with her family.

Sam and the rest of the funeral procession showed up and the services lasted for a little over an hour. There were several men at the funeral I didn't know. Sam said most were from the CIA and a few neighbors where Robert and Elle lived.

One of them stood out. He was bigger than most of the men; broad shoulders, muscular, salt and pepper hair. Maybe in his forties. I asked Sam who he was and he said his name was Karl Coleman. A former CIA operative that Robert trained.

"He's the Chief of Security for Armco International now, a munitions company owned by Elton Parker, another CIA operative Robert worked with in the sixties."

To my surprise Coleman came over and introduced himself. "My name's Karl, with a K, Coleman," he said. He grinned and extended a huge hand toward me.

"Clark McKay," I said. We shook hands. My hand almost disappeared in his. This was the guy that came to see Mr. Morgan.

"I understand you're an old Army buddy," he said, holding my hand like it was a grape he was about to crush.

"I've known the Spiciers for a long time," I said, retrieving my hand.

Sam stuck a cigarette in his mouth, put his hand in his pocket searching for a light. Coleman reached in his pocket, took out a book of matches and lit Sam's cigarette. The match cover had Twisted Lizard Gentleman's Club on it. He dropped the struck match on the ground and put the book back in his pocket.

"Thanks for the light," Sam said.

Coleman nodded. "Well, I've got to go," he said. "Nice to meet you, Clark. Maybe we can have a drink some time and trade stories about Spicier."

"Yeah, maybe so."

We shook hands again and he was gone.

"Sam, how well do you know Karl Coleman?"

"Not very well, why?"

"Coleman had a book of matches from the Twisted Lizard Club and so did the hoodlums that tried to kill me. Don't you think that's a little too coincidental?"

"Not really. Lots of men like to watch naked women. Even me sometimes."

"You've been there?"

"Once or twice a few years ago. Typical strip joint. A lot of horny men, strippers who double as whores…nothing new."

"I don't know. Something about Coleman makes me nervous."

"Go home, Clark, before you get yourself killed. Besides, I hear Goodnight is pissed off at you any way, he's sure as hell not going to let you in on anything, and he might arrest you for what you did to those punks."

"Goodnight needs to get his shit together."

Sam grinned, took a deep drag on his cigarette and exhaled, smoke curling up around his face.

"I think I'll pay the Twisted Lizard a visit." I said.

While I was talking, Sam field-stripped his cigarette and took his clippers out and trimmed his nails. I wasn't sure he was listening.

"Did you hear what I said, Sam?"

"I heard you, every word. What you really said was 'I'm going to get myself killed and I want you to be a witness.' I know you're too hard-headed for me to change your mind." He took another Marlboro out of the pack and began feeling around in his pocket for a light. I left him still fumbling in his pocket and went to say goodbye to Sara.

As I walked by the graves of Robert and Elle, I saw a woman in a black dress with a veil over her face standing alone in front of the tombstones. Though I hadn't seen her in five years, I immediately knew it was Pepper. I walked up beside her and confirmed her identity.

"You did make it."

"Hello, Colonel. I didn't want to go through all the hand shaking and false crying crap."

"What about your family, Bobby and Sara. Don't you think you owe them some kind of apology for not showing up for the services?"

"I'm here for my mom and dad, not for old home week. Bobby and Sara could care less that I'm here."

"That's where I think you're wrong. Give them a chance. Because you haven't been close in the past doesn't mean you can't be now. Life's too short as they say."

"Colonel, you're always the optimist. I've got to go."

"Where are you going?"

"I'm on thirty days leave. I intend to find who killed my mom and Dad."

"That's not going to be easy in thirty days. Maybe we could work together."

"I don't think so. You'd just slow me down."

"I can still hold my own. Just ask those two guys in the hospital who assumed the same thing."

"Sorry about that," she said. "I apologize." She walked away, got in a red Sebring convertible and was gone.

She was right about one thing. Getting old is a combination of your mind and body not being on the same page. It's hard to recognize what you can and can't do when you start getting old. Most of the time it's the physical things. Your mind still thinks you can do everything you always did but your body says, "Have you lost your freaking mind? I can't do that anymore!"

8

After the funeral, Bobby had all the contents of the house picked up and sent to his aunt Sara's by a moving company, and put the house up for sale. I convinced him to go back to his girlfriend and his computer programming job in L.A. If anyone bothered him I told him to call me. He left the Lincoln with me and took an afternoon flight back to L.A.

It was time to visit the Twisted Lizard. It was Saturday, all the strippers and perverts would be in attendance. Maybe Coleman would be there.

It started raining. The rain turned to sleet and the mixture made it difficult to see the lanes. A late-model black Mustang with two men in it kept showing up behind me, too often to be a coincidence. I could never get a good look at them. The rain and sleet kept obscuring my view. I made a block and came back to the same street. The Mustang was still there. I tried to read the license number. I finally got it but didn't have a pen to write it down.

The traffic light in front of me turned yellow. I slowed down to catch the red. At the last moment I accelerated through the light, hoping the Mustang would stop; they ran the light and caught up to me in the next block.

There was an alley coming up to my right. I waited until I was directly across from it, slammed on my brakes and made a ninety degree turn. The Mustang hit his brakes and a loud screeching sound made me wince as he slid down the dirty sleet-covered street.

That was the sound Mr. Morgan heard. I was sure of it. I made a right turn at the next corner and then two more rights, hoping to come up behind him. No Mustang. Whatever they had in mind didn't happen.

I called Sam. "I think I just saw Robert and Elle's killers," I said.

"Really?" he said.

"Yeah, they've been following me in a black Mustang but I lost them."

I could hear him blowing smoke. "You lost who, Clark?"

"Two men in a Mustang. Their brakes squeaked, like Mr. Morgan said he heard the night Robert and Elle were murdered."

"You're not making any sense, Clark. Where are you?"

I looked at the street sign. "South Albright. The 900 block."

"Okay, calm down," he said. "I want you to meet me at Nicklebacks. Go south one more block and turn left, you'll see a sign on your right about two or three blocks down the street. I'll be there as soon as I can. Wait for me and you can tell me all about it. It's a hangout for cops. You should be alright there. Tell Twinkle to put what you have on my tab."

"What kind of bar did you say it was?" I heard Sam laugh.

"A cop bar. The bartender has a gold front tooth that twinkles so we call him Twinkle."

"Sam is there something you're not telling me?" I asked.

"Just go," he said.

"If you say so. See you there," I said.

I made a left turn at the next block and saw a big, bright red and blue sign a few blocks down the street flashing 'NICKLEBACKS BAR & GRILL.' I found a place to park on the street and eased the Lincoln up behind a sea green Beetle convertible and walked back to an oversized red door.

The smell of stale beer and thick smoke hit me like a shithouse door as I walked in. I gasped and fought to get a good breath. I did a little stutter step and sneezed as I entered.

I saw four men a little long in the tooth dressed like Sam. Two were playing pool and two were eating burgers and drinking beer.

Empty beer bottles covered a large table across from the two pool tables. A jukebox was playing the Roger Miller classic "Dang Me." The bar was what the party-goers might call intimate, although I doubted if there were many parties. It looked more like a dropping-off place for tired old drunks. I should fit right in.

The exception was a pretty blonde woman wearing tight jeans and a pullover red sweater parked on a barstool at the end of the bar drinking a martini with two olives.

She gave me a look that made me check my zipper and went back to watching the pool players. I made my way to a barstool and sat down with my back to the bar.

I heard a man's gruff voice ask what I wanted to drink. "You got Jack Daniels?" I asked, turning around on the stool.

A big man wearing an apron was staring at me. He had red garters on the sleeves of a long-sleeve white shirt and a red bow tie. His thick, bushy eyebrow looked like you could mow 'em. He had wavy black hair parted in the middle and a black handlebar barbershop-quartet-looking mustache. I expected him to break into song any minute.

"Yeah I got it," he said, showing his twinkling gold front tooth with a not-too-happy face. "You want anything with it?"

"How about a glass of ice," I said. He reached under the bar and got a fifth of black label and sat it on the bar. He laid his hand on the bar, palm up. "Thirty bucks," he said.

"I can buy it down the street for eighteen," I said.

"Then go buy it down the street, but you can't bring in here to drink."

"How much is the ice?"

"The ice is free."

"What a deal."

"You want it or not?" he said.

I dropped two twenties in his hand. He laid a ten on the bar, filled a glass with ice and sat it in front of me. "Take it easy on that stuff while you're in here. I could lose my license for selling you a bottle." I nodded and he walked down the bar and started talking to the pretty lady.

After four shots of Jack, Sam showed up about the time I was considering calling him. He came over and set down.

One of the beer drinkers staggered up to Sam and grabbed his arm. "How you doing, Sammy boy?" he said.

"Pretty good, Bill," Sam said, turning away to escape his breath.

Bill was a little bigger and heavier than Sam. His suit was wrinkled with a beer stain on his shirt. His gray hair was falling down in his eyes and thick gray stubble covered his sagging face. If he had been on the street I would have donated a dollar. "I put my retirement papers in last week," he said. "I was forced out. They said I had a drinking problem. Who wouldn't have a drinking problem after thirty years with that bunch? I was a good cop." He burped, ordered another round for everyone in the bar, locked at the bottle of Jack in front of me and shook his head. "You can drink your own." He slapped Sam on the back and staggered back to his table.

Sam took a Marlboro out of his pocket and lit it. 'Okay, Clark," he said. "What's this about a Mustang?"

"I don't think I would be telling people I hang out at a place with a bartender named Twirkle," I said.

Sam shook his head and grinned. "It's a joke, Clark. We call him that as a joke."

"I know it's a joke, but on who?"

"Can we talk about the Mustang now?" he asked.

"Sure," I said. "I had a late-model black Mustang following me. I made a quick turn and when the Mustang hit his brakes to make the turn, there was a loud screeching metal to metal sound. That's the sound Mr. Morgan described to me as the one he heard the night Robert and Elle were killed. The killer or killers were in a hurry backing out of Robert's driveway. When they slammed on the brakes they locked up and made the sound Mr. Morgan heard. They didn't fix it and it did it again when they were chasing me. If we can find the Mustang, we may have the killers."

"Who's this Mr. Morgan you're talking about?"

"He's Robert's next door neighbor. Him and his wife are the ones who found them. I wrote the license number down but I'm not sure I remembered it right."

"You're sure about the Mustang?" Sam asked.

"I'm sure about the Mustang, not so sure about the license number. The only thing that puzzles me is why the dog was barking after the killers left," I said. "I haven't figured that out yet. Mr. Morgan insists the dog didn't start barking until thirty minutes after he heard the screeching sound. They were long gone by then."

"This is getting more confusing by the minute," Sam said. "What does the dog barking have to do with the Mustang?"

"Don't know. The dog didn't bark until they were gone. That doesn't make sense."

"Maybe he had his times mixed up," Sam said.

"The dog?" I grinned.

"Very funny," Sam said.

"Sorry, I couldn't resist."

"Can you identify the men in the Mustang?" Sam asked.

"Didn't get a good look at them, it was sleeting. Saw their ties and white shirts, though. Could have been CIA, FBI, or the police."

"Or maybe somebody wearing ties," Sam said. "You're guessing, Clark, it could have been anybody."

"That's true, but if we find the Mustang I'll bet we have the killers. You run that number and whoever owns that car has a lot of explaining to do."

"You're probably right," Sam said grinning. "Maybe I underestimated you."

"I just want to find who murdered Robert and Elle Sam."

"Did Robert say anything to you that might give us a clue to why someone would want to kill him?" Sam said. "Like something he had or gave you that pissed somebody off big time?"

"Not that I can remember. The only clue I have is those two idiots that tried to kill me. After seeing the Mustang I know that's got to be part of it."

Sam paused, lit another cigarette off of the one he still had in his hand. He rubbed the fire out of the old one with his hand and dropped it in an ashtray.

"I called a friend of mine to pick you up and take you to a safe house for tonight," Sam said. "After what you told me, I think it's the right thing to do. I'll have a tow truck take the Lincoln to the FBI compound. You can pick it up later."

"You sure that's a good idea? What about my things at the motel? I haven't checked out. Besides, I can take care of myself."

"Well, humor me. It won't be the first time I've saved your ass."

"True. I can remember two or three times very vividly. Who's this guy I'm waiting for?"

"His name is Cleaver. You sit tight and wait for him. It may be a while, but he'll be here. I got something I have to do, you wait. I'll see you tomorrow."

"I don't like it, but okay," I said.

Sam shook his head, waved goodbye to his drunk friend and left.

An hour later, I had drank about half the bottle of Jack when Twinkle asked one of the pool players to drive the drunk home and the pretty lady left shortly afterward, alone.

No one came in. It was just me, Twinkle and the two pool shooters.

The two remaining men put their pool cues away and moved to barstools a few seats from me and nodded hello. I returned the nod. They sat down and continued to drink beer.

I never understood how anyone could drink that much beer. It looked like horse piss to me. Whereas well-brewed whiskey was a different thing, and you didn't have to drink near as much to get rip-roaring drunk.

9

As I waited, my mind began to wander and I found myself breaking out in a cold sweat, thinking about Mary's car wreck. The front door opened and a man walked in. He wasn't dressed like the others, but by the way he came in you knew he and bars were old friends.

He was stocky built, under six foot, had a nose that looked like it had been broken a couple of times. He was almost bald, maybe in his fifties. He had on a white t-shirt under an open khaki jacket and jeans. I could see the butt of a .38 strapped to his belt. Except for the .38, he looked more like a truck driver that came in for a beer.

Twinkle must have been listening to me and Sam because he pointed to me.

The man nodded a thank you and walked over to the bar.
"You Clark?" he asked.

"Yes. And you're Cleaver, right?"

"Right," he said. "Let's go."

"Not even a hello," I said.

"Don't have time for hellos."

"Cleaver your first name or your last?"

"Just Cleaver," he said and gave me a sour look.

"Well, just Cleaver, where are we going?"

"You'll find out when we get there. Sam said to take care of you. I can do it better if you keep quiet."

"You FBI?" I asked, ignoring his comment.

"No, private eye. I help Sam out once in a while. Let's go."

I slid off the bar stool, put the top on my Jack and picked up the bottle. "Okay lead on," I said.

His car was an older-model Dodge Intrepid that needed a paint job. We made several hide and seek moves to check for a tail, left the highway ten miles outside of town, turned on an unmarked, one-lane blacktop road that ran two or three miles through the woods across a railroad track and came to a dead end in front of a log cabin. The cabin looked like it had been built from one of those kits you see advertised.

Cleaver told me to wait in the car. He got out with a flashlight, and made his way to a breaker box and turned on the electricity. The porch light came on and a nearby owl voiced his objection from one of the large trees that surrounded the cabin.

Cleaver unlocked the door to the cabin and turned on the lights.

"You've been here before, huh?"

"A couple of times. Me and Sam come up here to get away from people who talk too much."

The cabin was musty and my asthma began to act up. I opened a window and Cleaver walked over and slammed it down. "We have to keep the windows locked," he said. "Turn on the A/C if you need air."

"Do you think a locked sixteenth-of-an-inch-thick glass would keep anyone out if they really wanted to get in?"

"No, but most likely I would hear the glass break."

I pondered his answer, dismissed the logic and turned on the AC, although it was too cold in the cabin already.

There were two small beige-colored bedrooms, with identical double-beds, dressers and end tables in each room. They looked like motel rooms.

There was a small kitchen and bathroom across the hallway. An all-purpose room with the same color walls as the bedrooms was the largest room in the cabin. An artificial white bearskin rug lay on the hardwood floor beneath a coffee table in front of a red leather sofa with a TV, dining table and chairs on the other side of the room. I asked whose cabin it was and Cleaver said it was a friend of Sam's. He didn't know his name.

"I didn't think it was Sam's. He bitched for a year in Vietnam about the heat and jungles. Swore if he made it home he would never get close to anything green again and not more than ten feet from an air conditioner."

We sat and listened to an occasional train pass on the nearby tracks, played a few hands of Texas Hold-Em and talked about our mutual friend Sam. Cleaver said he met Sam ten years ago when Sam hired him to get the goods on his cheating wife. I knew about the ex-wife but I had never heard Sam say anything about his family. He never wanted to talk about it. Cleaver said Sam told him he grew up in Nevada and had a younger sister there. That's all he knew. That was more than I knew. I poured another stiff drink and downed it in one gulp. Cleaver looked at me and shook his head.

"What, you don't drink?" I asked.

"Not anymore," he said.

"What made you quit?"

"I don't want to talk about it."

"Okay, guess I'll have another and turn in," I said.

"Always another drink," he said. "It won't make your problems go away, it only makes them worse."

"I thought you didn't want to talk about it."

"I don't, but watching you, I see myself 10 years ago," he said.

"You don't know what I've been through. Everyone is always giving me advice."

"I'm not giving you advice. I'm telling you the truth."

"You don't know the pain I've had."

"Maybe I do."

"What happened to you, a nasty divorce?" I asked.

"No. It's a long story," he said.

"We got nothing but time."

"Okay, I'll tell you if I can. Ten years ago my only child was kidnapped, raped and buried alive. It sent my wife to an insane asylum and I stayed drunk for the next ten years. Then one night when I was in a stupor I started having hallucinations, seeing pink elephants and such, when suddenly my eight-year-old little girl was standing in front of me with tears in her eyes, holding her favorite teddy bear. 'Daddy, don't drink anymore,' she said. 'It won't bring me back.' I reached out for her but she was gone. I fell to my knees and cried until I passed out. When I woke up the next morning her teddy bear was lying on the bed. I almost had a heart attack. She had the bear with her when she was kidnapped. I think it was a miracle. I never took another drink."

"You quit cold turkey?"

"The shock cured me. I haven't had a drink since."

"That's hard to believe," I said.

"Believe what you want. Maybe you're not worth saving," he said. "I'm going to bed."

He walked away. I took one more shot of Jack, staggered to my look-alike bedroom, passed out and went to Vietnam as I often did.

I could feel the heat, the sweat, the bugs on my skin... As we approached a little village called Tresong, kids held out their hands for candy and cigarettes. The village chief and two orange-robed monks with beetle juice covering their teeth came out to greet us. They seemed friendly enough and offered us food and tea. We declined the food, but accepted the monk's tea. It would have been disrespectful not to. The village chief invited us into his hut. It smelled like chickens, garlic and smoke. The tea tasted like bird shit, which was what it was, and the conversation was nil, but we began to relax. The dirt floor moved and a little man with a big gun popped out of a hole beneath the hooch. The weapon barked and my face turned wet and warm as bullets whizzed past my head, streaking my executive officer. In an instant, I was wearing his blood and brains. I rolled away and got off two rounds with my .45 before the VC could turn his weapon on me. More blood and brains. I wanted to throw up but I didn't have time. I crashed through the bamboo straw of the hooch and tumbled into a pigpen full of shit. The rest of my "A-Team" scattered like a covey of quail when they heard the gunshots. After a five-minute firefight we managed to cut down several of the VC, and the rest disappeared into the jungle. We didn't go after them. It was their briar patch. They probably had booby traps waiting for us. As we looked around the village for any remaining VC we discovered three men, their hands tied behind their backs, shot execution-style in the back of the head. They were the real village chief and monks. Bodies of men women and children were scattered around in the nearby jungle like cord wood. My radio man was sitting against a push cart. He looked like he was wearing a red scarf. As I got closer the scarf turned into blood, his throat was cut. The air was full of the stench of death; it made the back of my tongue taste like rust.

I felt wet and woke up in my little bedroom, shaking, drenched in sweat. As usual, after the nightmares I had a migraine and a head full of ghosts.

It took a few minutes for me to come back to reality, and when I did, I didn't like it any better than the dream.

10

I made my way to the kitchen looking for something to eat and found a note Cleaver left. He said he went to the store to get food. I found a can of beanie weenies, blew the dust off the can and pulled the tab. They smelled and tasted better than I remembered.

The phone rang. It was Sam. "How you doing Clark?"

"Well, let's see. I've had a can of beans to eat in the last twenty-four hours. I lost twenty bucks to Cleaver in a card game. I'm tired from no sleep, reliving some of our escapades in Nam. Cleaver went to the store. He's probably chowin' down on a big steak while I sit here like Daniel Boone starving to death."

"Cleaver's gone?" Sam asked

"What did I say? He went to the store."

"You must be out of booze."

"Get me out of here, Sam, this was a mistake. I don't need anyone trying to repent me."

"What're you talking about?" Sam said.

"Clever told me some sob story about his little girl I'm sure he made up with your help."

"It's the truth, Clark. He never talks about it. I told him what happened to your wife and son. He must have thought he could help," Sam said. "You sure Robert never said anything about what kind of trouble he was in, or what he may have that someone wanted?"

"No. I'll apologize to Cleaver and have him drive me back to town," I said. "I got to get out of here." The sound of a car engine interrupted me. "Cleaver's here, Sam, got to go."

"Stay where you are," Sam said.

"Bye," I said and hung up.

I looked out the window. Cleaver's car rolled to a jerking stop in front of the cabin, the engine still running. I couldn't see anyone in the car, no one outside of it. I waited a few seconds, opened the cabin door and rushed down the steps to the Dodge.

I saw Cleaver lying on the front seat. His right hand wrapped around his .38 revolver. His left squeezing the steering wheel. A bullet hole in the driver's window had made a sunburst pattern as it blasted through the window into Cleaver. He was bleeding on the left side, just below the shoulder. He was still alive but leaking all over the car seat. The smell of gun powder filled the car. I took off my shirt, rolled it and tied it over the wound. It was like trying to plug a hole in the Hoover Dam with a cork; the blood wouldn't stop. I twisted the shirt into a tourniquet and it finally slowed to a trickle.

"Cleaver, you hear me?" He didn't answer. "Cleaver, who did this?"

He rose up on one elbow, pulled himself up closer with the steering wheel. "Mercedes...be here soon...go," he said and passed out, his hand still holding the wheel.

I removed his left hand from the steering column, swiped the glass from the seat with my hand, lifted him into the passenger seat and buckled the belt, and slid in behind the wheel. I pried the .38 from his hand. It was empty. I searched his coat and pants. No bullets, I was up shit creek without a paddle. There was no way I could get past them without firepower. The forest on both sides of the road was too dense to drive through. The train tracks, that was the only way. If I could get to them before the Mercedes I would have a chance to get to a crossing, get to the highway. Survival was a case of the first one to the railroad tracks

I jerked the Dodge in gear and put the pedal to the metal. The old Dodge hesitated then leapt onto the black top, digging in the oil dirt, smoke curling up from the wheels. I drove like I was in the lead at the 500. I could see the tracks. And I could hear the Mercedes. If I could hear them they could hear me.

Then I saw them. A big, dark blue four-door was racing toward me. I leaned back and jammed the pedal as far as it would go. The Dodge squealed, shot forward and bounced on the tracks, chewing up the dirt like a hungry lion, seconds before the Mercedes. There were deep-cut ditches on both sides to hold the flood water. One mistake and I would be sitting at the bottom of one.

I looked in the side mirror. The Mercedes was close. The mirror read OBJECTS ARE CLOSER THAN THEY APPEAR. Not something I wanted to know.

Cleaver's Dodge was falling apart piece by piece. As I rounded a curve something flew off the car and rolled into the ditch. I heard a train whistle. "Oh, shit."

The train was bearing down on the road crossing. If the train made it to the crossing before I did the coroner would be picking the steering wheel out of my ass. I had no place to go but forward.

The Mercedes was swinging slightly to either side, looking for a way off. But all there was were deep drop-offs into the murky swamp water, and coming right at us was a few thousand pounds of hot rolling death.

I saw a head poke out the side of the train engine and heard the scream of locking brakes. The grinding of the wheels on the tracks made an eerie, devilish sound of steel on steel. Sparks jumped from the rails like flaming crickets. It wasn't going to stop in time and I wasn't going to make the crossing.

I took a quick glance in the rearview mirror. The Mercedes had caught up to me, nudging the back of my car, honking and waving for me to go faster. Their eyes looked as wide as subway tunnels. The man in the passenger seat raised a pistol to shoot and the driver knocked his hand down. If he shot me they sure as hell wouldn't make it.

As I raced to the crossing, I coaxed the last bit of speed from the Dodge and pulled a few feet ahead the Mercedes. I was close enough to read the numbers on the front of the train engine, 4652. Cleaver would never know what hit him. Me, I was going to have a couple of bad moments.

I glanced to my left. In the depression next to the crossing the tops of two oaks waved in the wind, beckoning me to take flight. It wasn't much, but it was better than swallowing steel. The train's speed made it now or never. I bounced the Dodge over the left rail, jerking the wheel out of my hands. I went airborne and crashed in to the tops of the trees. As the car fell, the train screeched by. Another coat of paint and I would have been a memory.

For a moment the Dodge teetered, hung in the limbs like a baby in a cradle swaying back and forth. I heard the Mercedes being recycled as it crashed into the front of the train. The sound of the impact and the screaming whistle were deafening.

The weight of the Dodge made the trees dip and growl. Limbs tore and ripped. The car shook, then dropped hard in a freefall to the road; blowing tires, popping out the windshield, knocking open the trunk, sending the spare tire sailing into a ditch and giving me a mouthful of airbag. Airbag or not, my shoulder felt like it had been hit with a jackhammer.

I leaned over in the seat, looking at Cleaver He was lying on the floorboard. His seatbelt had snapped; one leg in the seat and his head against the side of the door. I checked his pulse. He was breathing. I pulled myself out from under the airbag and stumbled out of the car.

I could still hear the crunching metal sound and see fire streaks coming from the front of the train as it pushed what was left of the Mercedes several hundred feet down the tacks, finally slowing to a stop. Suddenly the mangled Mercedes exploded, scattering pieces in all directions. What was left of the men in the Mercedes could probably be picked up with an eye dropper.

I took a deep breath, found my phone and called 911. The sign at the crossing gave the location as Farm Road 2228 at Railroad Crossing 46. They said they knew where I was…thank goodness.

I noticed a bag in the open trunk. Inside was a .357 Colt, with a box of ammo and more ammo for the .38. put the .357 ammo and Colt in the inside pocket of my jacket and zipped it up, left the .38 on the seat and waited.

I needed a drink bad.

11

An ambulance arrived in a little over ten minutes, put Cleaver on life support, put my arm in a sling, gave me a mild tranquilizer and some pain pills and a ride to the hospital. I still needed the whiskey but the pills helped. I called Sam.

I was sitting in the waiting room, wearing my zipped jacket and no shirt, having a cup of coffee when Sam arrived. I was calm thanks to medical science; otherwise I would have strangled him.

"You okay Clark?"

"Yeah, no thanks to you," I said. "Cleaver's the one in trouble. He's in surgery now. The doctor said it was touch and go. How the hell did those two guys know we were at the cabin, Sam?"

"We'll figure it out."

"Well while you're figuring, I think it'll add up to be one of your friends at Nicklebacks. You said you could trust those pool shooters. I don't think so. Somebody sold us out."

"I didn't tell them anything," Sam said.

"Well they must have been listening. Those two didn't find us by accident."

I heard a rapping sound on the tile floor and turned from Sam to the noise. A young motorcycle cop wearing shiny brown knee-high leather boots with boot pants stuffed into them was walking towards me. He stopped in front of me, placed his helmet under his arm and looked at me through mirrored sunshades. "Are you the one that was involved in the accident?" he asked.

"If you mean the train accident I am."

"You have to come with me sir."

"I have a friend in surgery that may die. I'll come later and fill out whatever forms you want me to."

"It's more than forms. You have to answer questions about the accident."

"I'm not going anywhere right now."

"I think you are, sir," he said, flipping the safety strap off the hammer on his revolver.

"Whoa there," Sam said. "What seems to be the trouble, officer?"

"Who are you?" the cop asked.

"FBI, Agent Sam Tuit." Sam reached in his pocket and took out his badge while pushing the officer's gun hand away from the gun with his other hand. Sam looked at the cop's name tag. "Officer Harper," he said, "Mr. McKay is working with me, it's alright."

The young man took off his shades and took a step closer to Sam, and with a half-whisper said, "I didn't know. I have to make a report, Agent Tuit. They sent me to bring him in."

"I know. It's okay, I need your help too."

"What do you want me to do, sir?"

"Well, for starters, what happened to the men in the Mercedes?"

"Dead. The train cut them up pretty bad. They're still trying to find all the pieces."

"Have you made an I. D. on them yet?"

"Yes sir we did." He pulled a small notebook from his pocket. "The driver was Edward Campos. From Chicago. The other man was Louis Sanfini from D. C."

The name Sanfini got my attention. Sanfini was the name of the muscle head I dealt with in Washington, but his first name wasn't Louis. Holy shit there's more than one of them. God made a serious mistake.

"What about the car?" Sam asked.

"The Mercedes was a rental from Arlington, Virginia. Mr. Wendell Overa rented the car from Atlas Auto Rentals yesterday morning. We haven't found him yet. He wasn't in the car and he wasn't at the address he put on the rental form."

"Anything else?"

"No sir."

"Good. That's all for now, Officer."

"What about Mr. McKay?"

"It's okay. I'll call your superior. Let's keep our conversation confidential for now."

"You sure it will be okay, Mr. Tuit?"

"Yes, it's okay."

"See you then," he said, turned away down the hall and was gone.

"I don't believe you did that, Sam." I said. "You're good."

"Forget it. I would have had to go to the station and get you out anyway."

The doctor came in, his surgeon's mask hanging around his neck. You knew from his movements he had done this many times before. His forehead was dotted with perspiration. He was of Mid-Eastern descent. He looked tired from too much work; his scrubs had blood on them.

"This is Sam Tuit, doctor. He's a good friend of the Cleavers," I said.

The doctor gave Sam a quick nod. "I'm sorry, Mr. Cleaver didn't make it. He lost too much blood and the bullet penetrated his lungs. I'll need a police release before I can give you the body."

"I'll take care of that doctor," Sam said. "I'm FBI."

The doctor nodded. "Sorry," he said again and left the way he came in.

"Damn it, Sam. If I could have gotten him here sooner, he may have made it. I didn't know him but I liked him."

"You did what you could. You need to get out of here. I'll take care of Cleaver. Take my car and go back to D.C. Your things are in the backseat. You can leave the car at Nicklebacks. I'll hitch a ride with a local cop and pick the car up later."

"Sam, what was Cleaver's other name? I never knew if Cleaver was his first or last name."

"His name was Albert Alfonso Cleaver. He didn't like his given name so he went by Cleaver."

"That is a load. I'll leave your car at Nicklebacks."

"If you need any money for Cleaver let me know."

"I'll do that," Sam said. "Now go."

12

I parked Sam's car in front of Nicklebacks, gave Twinkle the keys and caught a taxi to the FBI compound to pick up the Lincoln. They said they couldn't let me have it until Sam released it. I caught another taxi to a car rental place. I had just settled in when my cell phone rang. I picked it up and said hello.

"Hi Colonel, it's Pepper. I want to talk to you."

"Talk."

"No, I mean in person."

"You sure I can keep up?"

"I'm sorry about that. I was upset. Really, I'm very sorry."

"All right, come on. We'll talk. I'm at the Carroll Inn on Fourth Street."

"Good," she said, "I'll be there in about an hour," and hung up.

Sometime during the ten o'clock news I dozed off. A knock on the door woke me. I took a peek out the window and there stood Pepper in her Army uniform.

She gave me a sheepish smile as she walked in. "Thanks, Colonel, should I salute?"

"I'm retired, Captain. What are you doing in uniform? I thought you were on leave?"

"I am. I went to a 'Hail and Farewell.' Some of the guys I served with in Iraq were being discharged. I thought I should say goodbye."

"That was the right thing to do. Don't forget your comrades."

"I feel really bad about the last time we met."

"Grief can make you do foolish things," I said. "I know. What did you want to talk about?"

"I have a boyfriend that's an Army Major in intelligence. He was in Iraq with me. He's stationed at Fort Meade now. I asked him to find out what he could about my dad and the CIA and he said they were investigating dad for stealing some documents from the Company."

"Did your dad ever say anything to you about it?"

"No, nothing. If he did steal anything it would come as a surprise to me. He was a straight arrow always lecturing me and Bobby about right and wrong."

"That was my feeling," I said.

"Matt, that's my boyfriend, said he's sure about the investigation."

"I see. From your insignia you're in the Infantry. Why not JAG?"

"Thought I could be more useful as a soldier than a lawyer."

"Or be closer to that boyfriend of yours."

"Both."

"You going to marry him?"

"We've talked about it."

"No proposal?"

"It hasn't got to that yet."

"Bobby said you haven't talked to him in over a year. Why?"

"It's a family matter."

"He's my godson. I thought I was family."

"Okay. You want to know the truth, why do you think he's living in fairyland? He's gay, Colonel. It would have broken dad's heart if he had known, that's why I stayed away. I was afraid I would spill the beans"

"He's got a girlfriend."

"That's just a cover. She stays there to get free room and board along with his live-in male lover. I was in California last year and paid him a surprise visit. His partner, as he called himself, told me all about it."

"He's still your brother and he loves you."

"Yeah, along with some hairy-chested freak."

"I admit I'm shocked. I didn't have a clue. But he's still my godson and it's his life."

"I'm not ready to accept it. I told him I wouldn't tell anyone. Now I've blabbed it to you, he'll never forgive me."

"I think so. Times have changed. It's not like it used to be. He is who he is, we have to accept it. I wish he wasn't gay, but that's not going to change anything. I know this has been hard for you, Pepper. It took courage to come here. You and Bobby need to take care of each other."

"I'll try," she said.

"See what else Matt can come up with and let me know," I said.

"Colonel, don't tell Bobby I told you. I don't think he wanted you to know."

"He'll tell me when he's ready."

"I'll keep in touch," she said. "Let me know if you need anything."

"The same here," I said.

"I am sorry. You and my dad were always my heroes. Will you forgive me?"

"Let it go. I have."

"Bye," she said and I opened the door for her.

"Take care of yourself," I said.

She nodded and walked out the door.

13

I ventured into the Twisted Lizard about ten-thirty, paid a twenty-dollar cover charge and sat down. The main part of the club was one big room, maybe a hundred square feet with a half-moon stage and two fireman's poles in the middle of the stage for strippers to climb and gyrate on. Large photographic pictures of naked women in various poses hung on pink walls. Thirty or forty tables were filled with men hungry for the female body. A mixture of beer, cigarette butts and cheap perfume created a sweet pungent odor that hung in the room like a cloudy curtain. My asthma gave me fits but there was no turning back now.

A large, enclosed waterless aquarium with a verity of leafy foliage ran the length of the bar with an assortment of multicolored lizards moving about, snapping up insects.

Three well-endowed topless young ladies were tending bar. The walkway behind the bar was elevated so you were looking directly in to the g-string-clad crotch of the barmaid when she walked up to you. You didn't have to wonder if she shaved it. The one that came to my bar stool was maybe twenty, long blonde hair, blue eyes, a well-proportioned body and large breasts.

"What'll you have honey," she asked looking down at me, smiling.

"Jack and coke; light on the coke, heavy on the Jack," I said. She wrote it on her pad and bounced away.

The lights dimmed and a little man in a flowered short sleeve shirt came on stage and took a microphone from a stand. A spotlight zeroed in on him. He smiled and thumped the mic. He had stooped shoulders, large ears, thin hair on top and a braided ponytail past his shoulders. He was short, probably five-foot-one or two, under forty and a little overweight.

"Good evening, gentlemen. I'm the owner and host of the Twisted Lizard, Ticky Malone. Gather round because we have a great show for you tonight. Twenty of the most beautiful girls in the world will perform for you. The star of our show is the gorgeous Bombshell from Brazil, Dawn 'Sugar Lips' Sanchez. The girl with the snapping turtle, the super large hooters guaranteed to turn you on. I give you…Sugar Lips Sanchez!" The spotlight dashed across the stage to a closed curtain.

When the curtain opened, a tall beautiful woman emerged. A thunderous applause echoed around the room as she rushed on stage. Men stood up and whistled.

She wore black leather shorts, black shiny stiletto high heels and a black leather vest that covered most of her huge, perfectly-shaped breasts. Her body was firm and smooth. Long, black wavy hair fell across her shoulders. She wore heavy make up on big brown eyes, and her long fingers were accented by sharp manicured pink nails. She moved with cat-like grace to a fire pole, grasped it with both hands and turned upside down, spread her legs parallel to the pole then pulled them back together and circled the pole with her body, sliding down to the floor. She sat snug against the pole, spread her legs again and lifted them back over her head, rolled over to her feet and stood up. The crowd went wild.

She removed the shorts, showing a tight rounded derriere, discarded the vest to expose hard nipples extending from her large breasts. She crawled across the stage on all fours, pulling her g-string open every few feet to give the crowd a look at what they came to see. The applause became deafening. She circled the stage again and again, gyrating her assets toward every man on the front row. Soon the crowd was worked into a frenzy. Men were putting money in her g-string and throwing it on stage from all over the room. One man tried to climb on stage; a bouncer quickly grabbed him and slammed him back down in his seat. She knew how to push all the right buttons to get a man excited. Her act lasted about thirty minutes. She would perform again later.

After her act, a variety of busty young women paraded across the stage performing for the totally-male audience. None generated the excitement of Sugar Lips Sanchez.

A little later, two men came in and cornered Malone and were giving him hell about something. The bigger of the two had a hold of his arm and the other one was in his face. Malone jerked away and went behind the bar and handed the big man an envelope. They apparently got what they came for and left without staying for any of the performances.

Blondie finally brought my drink. I asked her if she knew Karl Coleman. She said he was a friend of Sugar Lips. I gave her a twenty and she stood there until I gave her five more to go away. These girls probably made more than a congressman. Well maybe not that much, counting bribes, but a lot.

Sugar Lips performed again with the same results.

She put her shorts and vest back on and made the rounds on the floor. She finally got to me. "Hi," she said with a big smile. "I don't remember seeing you here before."

"That's because I haven't been here before."

She blinked her big brown eyes and gave me a phony laugh.

"What's your name, honey?" she asked, sitting down beside me.

I didn't know if I should tell the truth or lie. I didn't have this detective thing down yet. Before I could answer her question she was rubbing her leg against mine.

"Walker, Mike Walker," I said. I wasn't sure why I told her that. It just came out. Maybe it was because I was thinking naughty thoughts and wanted it to be someone else.

"Mike you going to be in town for long?" she said.

"I don't know. I was looking for a guy that comes in here. His name is Karl Coleman. The bartender said you knew him." Her smile went away and she moved her leg.

"You a friend of Karl's?" she said with a touch of sarcasm.

"Well, not exactly a friend. More like an acquaintance. He invited me to have a drink with him."

"Karl only comes around when he wants something."

"I don't know him very well. I'll take your word for it."

"I hate him, he's nothing but trouble."

"What did he do?"

"I don't want to talk about him anymore. I've got to go." She jumped up, rushed past several men trying to grab her and disappeared from the bar into the strippers lounge.

Malone saw her leave in a hurry and came over. "You and Sugar Lips okay, mister?"

"Yeah, fine. We were discussing the price of tea in China when she suddenly remembered she left the tea pot on."

It took him a couple seconds to get it, he wasn't too happy when he did. "Was that supposed to be funny?"

"What else would hookers talk about at one in the morning?"

"She's not a hooker, she's a show girl."

"Yeah and I'm the Pope."

"You're not from around here, are you?"

"You're a very astute little man. I came in to see if Karl Coleman was here."

"Coleman's not here. He may not be back. We had a little misunderstanding."

"Was it about the way Sugar Lips made tea?"

"You're a regular Rodney Dangerfield, aren't you?"

"I try," I said, shrugging my shoulders. "I try."

"Vinnie," Malone said, motioning for one of his bouncers.

That was my cue to leave. I threw a twenty on the bar and walked away. Malone was still watching me when I turned and looked back to give him a big wave as I left.

I waited in my car for the club to close and kept dozing off. It was way past this old man's bed time.

A car starting woke me. It was Sugar Lips, and she was alone. She pulled out in the street. I followed at a safe distance.

She stopped at a convenience store, picked up something and turned on the next street, pulled into the driveway of a small house and used a key to get in. I wrote down the address and headed for Mike Walkers motel. I would see her tomorrow.

14

I woke around ten, had a double shot of Jack and drove to Sugar Lips' place. She said she hated Coleman. That meant she knew him well. A woman's scorn and all that stuff.

About an hour later I parked the rental on the street where I could make a fast get away. Her old BMW was outside. I walked up to the door and rang the bell three times. Through a crack in a Venetian blind I saw her moving to the door. She was naked except for her house shoes. She peeked through the blind. "Go away," she said and disappeared.

I rang the bell several more times before she returned to the door, this time wearing a robe.

"I told you to go away," she said, "you a cop? You know you're supposed to identify yourself."

"No, I'm not a cop. We met at the club last night. I want to talk to you about Coleman, I think he may know something about a friend of mine's murder."

"What's that to me, I don't know anything about a murder."

"I'm not saying you do. Let me in, I'll explain."

There was a long pause.

"Do I know you?" she asked.

"Like I said, we met at the club last night."

I heard the bolt slide. She cracked the door, the night latch still hooked. "You were at the Lizard last night?"

"Yes."

"So what?"

"I need your help. I won't take long."

She hesitated for a moment, unlatched the door and motioned with her head for me to come in. Her eyes were slits and the heavy makeup was gone, but she was still a pretty woman. She pulled the robe tighter around her with shaking hands and told me to sit down on a small green couch with clothes piled on it. After I squeezed in between all the girlie things I looked around.

The coffee table's glass top was cracked and cluttered with empty beer bottles, coke cans and hamburger wrappers, carpet stains on the floor; there were no pictures on the tables or walls. The white paint had turned to a sick gray. Soiled sheets covered the windows. The smell of dirty dishes forced their way through a half-open kitchen door to my unsuspecting nostrils and made a quick cough jump out. Not the kind of place that would get a good housekeeping seal of approval.

"Excuse me," I said. "Must be catching a cold."

She nervously ran her fingers through her long black hair. It was obvious she was still trying to figure out who the hell I was.

"I wanted to ask you about Karl Coleman."

"Hope I never see that ass hole again," she said.

"I won't take long," I said.

"You want some coffee?" she said, batting her sleepy eyes.

I nodded yes, even though I was up to my eye balls in coffee already.

She left, and was back in a minute and handed me a cup of lukewarm instant coffee. She sat down on the edge of the couch facing me, placed her coffee cup on the cracked table without taking a drink, coughed, wiped her nose with a Kleenex and crossed her legs, too late. She gave me a puzzled look and stared at me for a second or two. I saw the light come on. "You're the guy from out of town. I remember that cowboy voice."

"That's right. Clark McKay. From Trouville, Texas, at your service," I said with a big grin. I was glad she didn't remember the name.

"Never met a real live Texan before," she said and smiled through quivering lips.

"Now you have."

"I don't know where Karl is," she said.

"Tell me what you know about him," I said.

"Much more than I want to." Her lips were sticking together. "Would you ...excuse me...there's something I have to do." She got up and disappeared into the bedroom. It was more than ten minutes before she returned. A change had come over her. Her hands were not shaking and she had that Sugar Lips smile I had seen at the club.

"What do you want to know about that bastard," she said.

"Whatever you can tell me."

"Mister, I was clean for over four years when Karl showed up at the Lizard, force-fed me some nose candy and I've been back on the shit for a year now. You said something about a murder, you think Karl did it?"

"Maybe," I said.

"If he did it would be good to have some payback. I'll tell you what I know."

"How did you wind up at the Twisted Lizard?" I asked.

"You want to know about Karl or me?"

"Both."

"My old man sold me for two thousand dollars to a New York pimp when I was thirteen. That's a lot of money in Brazil. I got away and hitchhiked to D.C. I've been on my own ever since."

"Where does Malone fit in?"

"Ticky's just my boss. Who was the friend that was murdered?"

"An old Army buddy and his wife."

"Somebody snuffed both of them?"

"Yes."

"Karl used to be CIA. Did you know that?" she asked.

"That's how he knew my friend? What happened with you and Coleman?"

"We got in an argument at the club. He wanted me to leave with him. I didn't want to go. Ticky interfered, Karl slapped him and Ticky pulled a gun. Karl said he would see Ticky without his bodyguards and left. I haven't seen or heard from him since."

"How long has that been?"

"Maybe two weeks."

"Who were those two men giving Malone a hard time last night?"

"What two men?"

She must have been higher than a kite. I guess it helps if you're going to walk around naked in front of a hundred strange men. "The two that were following Malone around. You were on the floor, you saw them."

"Oh, yeah, I remember now. They work for Jimmy Sanfini."

"My god there's more Sanfinis?"

"You know the Sanfinis?"

"Kind of, how many are there?"

"As far as I know there's three. Louis, Jimmy and Louis's son Diego. Somebody beat the hell out of Diego, he's still in the hospital."

"I know, I'm that somebody."

Her eyes lit up and she seemed genuinely pleased. "Well I'll be damned. Karl said he hired Diego and his queer friend to kick somebody's ass and they were the ones that got the ass kicking." She gave me a big smile and seemed more relaxed. She apparently didn't know about Louis, so I didn't tell her. She took a sip of bad coffee, grimaced and sat the coffee cup back on the cracked table. "I knew there's was something about you I liked," she said. "I'm glad he finally got what was coming to him. He beat up a couple of the girls at the club and tried to hit on me. He thought his muscles made him sexy and all the girls were supposed to spread their legs when he said so, for free."

"Do you know if Jimmy Sanfini is connected to the mob?"

"I don't know much about Jimmy. I've seen him at the Lizard maybe twice in the year I've been there. His two men come around about once a week to see Ticky. Sometimes they give Ticky money and sometimes he gives them money, I don't know what for. Louis and Diego used to come in together almost every Saturday until you beat the hell out of Diego. I haven't seen Louis lately either."

"I don't think Louis will be back," I mumbled.

"What's that?"

"Nothing, did Coleman ever mention the name Robert Spicier."

"I don't think so."

"What else do you remember? It could be important."

"Let's see," she said, rolling her eyes. "Nothing comes to mind. This is not one of my better days." She reached into her housecoat pocket, took out a bag of cocaine and put a pinch in her nose and took a deep breath. Her eyes rolled back in her head. She snorted and looked at me with a dazed expression. "You want a hit?" she asked.

"No thank you. I have enough trouble with the booze. I don't need to add something else. I think it's time for me to go. Thanks for the information, Sugar Lips."

"My name's Dawn. That Sugar Lips and Brazil shit is for the suckers at the Lizard. I might've been born in Brazil, but I couldn't find it on a map."

15

After I left Sugar Lips' I headed back to the motel. Goodnight called and asked if I could come by the station, he wanted to talk to me about a new development in the case. He asked if I could bring Pepper and I said okay.

I called Pepper and told her to meet me at Goodnight's office, he had some news about her dad and mom.

We walked past Sergeant Baldona and nodded hello. Baldona gave Pepper the big eye and we kept moving toward Goodnight's office. Pepper's high heels clicking on the tile floor sounded like rapid gun fire. The door was open. Goodnight was seated behind his desk. I could see the back of a man's head sitting in a chair across from Goodnight. As we entered the office the man stood up. He looked to be in his early thirties, well-built, thick shoulders, maybe a guy who played some football once. The butt of a gun poked out from under his open coat.

"Rick Terrell," he said, extending his hand.

"Clark McKay." We shook hands.

"And this pretty lady is?" Rick asked, turning toward Pepper.

"Amanda Spicier. Robert's daughter," I said. "We call her Pepper."

"Well she's certainly a pepper-upper. I knew he had a daughter, I didn't know how pretty she was. I'm sorry about your mom and dad Amanda."

"Thank you," Pepper said.

"Have a seat," Goodnight said, pointing at two empty chairs. "Miss Spicier, please." He offered Pepper the softest-looking chair.

Goodnight seated himself after we all sat down and looked at Rick. "Rick works for the CIA," Goodnight said.

"You knew my dad?" Pepper asked, looking at Rick.

"Yes. Robert talked about his family and he had a lot of war stories about the two of you, Colonel. Maybe you can tell me which ones are true."

"If he told you about them they were all true."

Goodnight and Terrell looked at each other but said nothing.

"I came here because I wanted to ask you some questions about Robert. Forgive me, Miss Spicier, if I get personal - it's my job," Terrell said.

"What's that?" Pepper asked.

"Robert was working on archive files for storage," Rick said. "He was very bored with it and amused himself by trying to mentally solve some of the cases before reading the conclusion of the file. I didn't think anything about it at the time. Now in hindsight it may have had something to do with his death."

"I thought it was supposed to be a suicide?" I said.

"Maybe," Rick said. He looked at Goodnight like he had let the cat out of the bag.

"Regardless," he said. "Some files are missing. I don't know if Robert took them but we need them back. If you know anything about them you need to tell me. It could be a criminal offense to withhold information."

"What kind of files?" Pepper asked."

"They contained information that could affect the security of our country. Information that could compromise military intelligence."

"What makes you think we would know anything about it?" I said.

"Families share secrets. Do you know anything I should know?"

"Too bad Robert's not here to defend himself," I said.

Terrell stood up. "I have to go now. If you find out anything about the file call me." He handed me and Pepper a card, turned toward the door then stopped and turned back to face us. "Oh, just out of curiosity, why did Robert insist on being called Robert instead of Bob or Bobby?"

"Because that was his name," I said.

Terrell looked at Goodnight like, *can I kill this guy*, turned and left.

Goodnight flopped back down in his seat and gave me a frown. "Did you have to insult the man?"

"I don't like him. There's something about him that rubs me the wrong way."

"That goes for me too," Pepper said. "He gives me the creeps."

Goodnight shook his head. "I think the feeling is mutual," Goodnight said and picked up a folder from his desk and opened it.

It looked like the same folder he had before, although all manila folders look alike to me.

"We got the toxicology report back," he said. "Miss Spicier, you can pass this on to your brother. Someone injected trichloroethylene in the air system of the house. It's an industrial solvent, more commonly known as Trilene. It's very effective as an anesthesia. It's quick acting and doesn't take much to render a person unconscious for a short period of time. It dissipates very quickly. That's the evidence we needed to change the case from a suicide/murder to a homicide. You were right, Colonel, it was murder."

"I never had any doubt," I said.

"Lieutenant Goodnight," Pepper said, "you caused a lot of anxiety and heartache in my family with your suicide/murder theory." She slid forward in her chair and gave Goodnight that same cold family expression I saw Bobby give him when we first met. "I suggest you have all your facts before you go off halfcocked in the future. You and the department could find yourself on the wrong side of a lawsuit. I say that as a lawyer, not a daughter."

Goodnight looked at Pepper, took off his glasses, pitched them on his desk, leaned back in his chair and shook his head in agreement. "I had that coming, counselor. I can admit when I'm wrong and I think I have a clue on who was involved. Rick and I were discussing the MO before you got here. He said that this was a method used by the CIA to give the impression an assassination was suicide. A man named Karl Coleman was especially adept at using it."

"I met him at the funeral," I said.

"He also said Mr. Spicier and Coleman had been having some hard feelings over something and Coleman had threatened Mr. Spicier."

"Why would Terrell want to implicate Coleman unless he had something to gain from it?"

"Maybe he wanted to help," Goodnight said.

"I doubt it."

"I'm going to issue a probable cause warrant for Coleman," Goodnight said. "We'll pick him up and see if he knows anything. I'm sorry about your friend and I'm sorry I didn't believe you."

"The Trilene explains why the dog was barking after the brake sound," I said. "He was unconscious too."

"What brake sound?" Goodnight asked.

"The sound that Mr. Morgan heard. He said he told you about it."

"He didn't say anything about a brake sound, just that he heard a noise. I never took it seriously."

"Well you should have. Didn't Sam tell you about the Mustang that was following me? The squeaking brakes?"

"I haven't talked to Sam since he called me right after the Spiciers were killed."

"That's strange, he seemed so emphatic about telling you, saying it was your case, professional ethics. He was going to talk to you the next day. That was two days ago."

"I haven't talked to him about the Mustang or anything else."

"Why would Sam tell me that? He said he talked to you."

"I don't know. I'm sure there's an explanation."

"I wish I knew what it was."

"When we find Sam I'll ask him. In the meantime I'll see what Coleman has to say about all this."

"Lieutenant, do you think Coleman murdered my parents?" Pepper asked.

"I need facts, Miss Spicier, all the facts as you reminded me. Then we will know."

"Did you know Coleman sent those two thugs after me?" I asked.

"Yeah, I heard about that. How do you know it was Coleman?" Goodnight said.

"I have a witness that heard him say he was pissed off at Sanfini and Sloan for messing up a job he gave them. That job was me."

"You're lucky they didn't press charges," Goodnight said.

"They came after me, Lieutenant. I had to defend myself."

"Who's your witness?"

"Dawn Sanchez. Works at the Twisted Lizard."

"I'm afraid she's not a very credible witness. We've picked her up for prostitution and drugs three or four times. A judge is not going to take her testimony seriously."

"Lieutenant Goodnight's right, Colonel," Pepper said. "No one's going to believe her with a record like that."

"You're probably right. Just the same, I think Coleman's up to his neck in this, if he didn't pull the trigger he knows who did."

"That's why we want to talk to him. We know he has used the MO before for the CIA"

"My guess is it's the men in the Mustang. Since Sam didn't give you the number I'll write it down for you." I picked up a pen and a sticky note pad from his desk. "Here's the license number." I laid the pad on his desk. He took a quick look and pushed it aside.

Pepper picked the pad up and put it in his hand.

"Check it out," she said, giving him that stare again.

Goodnight swung a finger, pointing at both of us. "You sure you're not related?" he said.

Pepper looked at me, smiled and patted my hand. "We probably are," she said and I smiled too.

Part 2
The File

16

I walked Pepper to her car. "Colonel, tell you what," she said, "I'm not the best cook in the world but I would like to fix dinner for you. Kind of a peace offering."

"There's no need for that. I'm fine."

"Well let's do it anyway. I'll see if Matt can come. I want you to meet him."

"Okay, let me know when," I said.

"Good. I'll call you in the next day or two. In the meantime you can stay at my place if you like. Save a lot of motel bills."

"Thanks. I appreciate that, but after five years I'm used to it."

"Thought I would make the offer." She smiled, got in her red convertible and drove away.

A white cargo van pulled out of the parking lot when I did. It was still behind me ten blocks later. It was time for the old double-back trick to find out if I was being followed.

I made a right turn at the next corner and two more right turns, the van was still there. I punched the horses and separated myself. A few seconds later the van was back. He pulled alongside me. I hit my brakes and he shot by. I got a good look at the driver; it was Vinnie from the Twisted Lizard.

I turned the car across a foot-high median to the opposite lane going the other way. I tried to call 911 but the phone kept cutting out. The van jumped the median and was speeding towards me. It swerved around two cars, moved behind me and clipped the back of my car, spinning me around until I hit a curb, bounced off a street sign and hit a concrete retaining wall. That was the last thing I remembered until…

I woke up to Tom Jones singing *"What's new, pussycat,"* the music vibrating through the walls. A blurred figure standing over me slapped me hard, snapping my head back. When the fog cleared I saw Malone and Vinnie giving me the evil eye.

I was sitting in a chair, my hands cuffed behind me, a rope tied across my chest and my feet tied to the legs of a chair. It wasn't hard to figure out I was in Ticky Malone's office and in a world of shit.

"You feel like cracking some jokes, funny man?" Malone said. Both men began to laugh.

"Just looking at you, little man, is enough to make anyone laugh."

"You sonofabitch," Malone said, slugging me in the eye. The little bastard had quite a punch. My ears were ringing, my eye swelling.

Malone's cell phone rang and I heard him say he would get whatever information they needed out of me one way or another. "Watch this guy, Vinnie," Malone said. "I have to go introduce Sugar Lips. If he tries anything, kill him."

"Yeah, Ticky. If he makes one sound I'll cut his throat." He pointed a crooked finger at me, showed a big smile and made a gargling sound as he ran his hand across his throat to show me what he would do. This guy had to be on the return to sender list. He had cauliflower ears, bulging brown eyes, receding black greasy hair combed straight back and a big flat nose that ran all over his face. He wore baggy pants and a shirt that looked like a Goodwill reject.

He checked my ties and looked at me like I was a hog in a packing plant, then drew a switchblade from his pocket and twirled the shiny blade in my face. "Why don't you try something, funny man. Give me a reason to carve you up. I would love to see you bleed."

I heard Sugar Lips' music and knew Malone would be back soon. Anything was better than being left with this nut.

Malone walked in and locked the door. He grabbed a straight-back chair, spun it around and camped on it backwards, facing me with his arms resting on the back of the chair. "Your name's McKay. That right?" Malone said.

"I thought his name was funny man, Ticky?" Vinnie said, puzzled.

"Vinnie, you dumb sonofabitch," Malone said. "How many fights did you have?"

"I don't know," Vinnie said, squinting through blank eyes. "I thought we were talking about this guy's name."

Malone looked at Vinnie, shook his head, took a deep breath and slowly exhaled, then turned back to me. "You see what I have to put up with McKay. Let's get this over with. I have a question for you. I want the right answer the first time. I don't have time for any bullshit stories." He was spitting on me through gapped teeth as he spoke. He grabbed me by the hair and jerked my head back. "Where's that damn file!?"

"I don't know what you're talking about."

He jumped up, took a step back from me, whirled and kicked me in the chest – sending me sliding across the floor, me and the chair bouncing off the wall and turning over on our side. Blood shot out of my nose and splattered on my shirt, my eyes blinking uncontrollably like a stop sign.

"Get him up, Vinnie," he said, shaking his finger at me.

Vinnie came over and sat me upright in the chair.

"Have I got your attention?" Malone said bending over, looking me in the face.

"Yeah, I hear you. I'm going to stomp your sawed-off ass when I get out of this chair."

"If you don't tell me where that damn file is I'll bury you in that chair." He began to walk in circles around me, his long ponytail swinging back and forth. "I owe the boys in Atlantic City a very large sum of money that they'll wipe clean when you tell me where the file is. If you don't I'll give you to Vinnie. He'll enjoy watching you suffer. It may take days for you to die."

"If you're talking about the file Robert Spicier was supposed to have taken I don't have it, never did. I don't give a shit about it, whatever it is."

Malone slapped me across the face and my nose started bleeding again. "You little no-good sack of shit. I hope they cut your balls off," I said.

Malone walked over to a desk, pushed the chair back and pulled a short barrel .38 S&W out of the drawer. A big fat black widow spider scampered out of the drawer, ran across the desk and down the leg. Even the spider knew it was time to haul ass. Malone walked up to me and cocked the hammer. "How about I just blow your head off," he said and placed the barrel between my eyes.

For some unknown reason I didn't understand. . .I
thought of the famous Eddie Adams photograph of the South
Vietnamese officer blowing a VC's head off in downtown
Saigon during the Tet Offensive. There was nothing that VC
could do but die. That's the situation I was in.

"Tell me what I want to know, now," Malone said.

"How are you going to find the file if you shoot me,
dumb ass?"

"They're going to kill me anyway if I don't come up with
it by morning. I might as well have the satisfaction of blowing
your shit away too."

"Shoot him, Ticky," Vinnie said, opening and closing his
fist. "Want me to cut him?" Vinnie reached in his pocket for
his knife.

"Shut up, Vinnie, let me think," Malone said. Sweat was
pouring down his face. He dropped the gun to his side and
began walking back and forth, the hammer still cocked. That
thing could go off at any time. The only thing keeping me
alive was the fact he didn't really know if I knew where the
file was.

"Okay," I said. "You win. Let me out of here and I'll give
up the file."

"Just tell me and I won't let Vinnie work on you. I'll make
it quick."

"No way. You leave Vinnie here and I'll take you to it."

"Vinnie goes," he said, shaking his head.

"You have the gun, why do you need Vinnie?"

"No deal, McKay. You're trying to pull something."
Malone stepped back and sat down on the corner of a daybed
that was probably used to interview new strippers. He kept
waving the gun towards me.

"Look, we're both in a jam," I said. "I'll give you the file,
it doesn't mean anything to me. You let me go. You get what
you want and I get out of this mess."

"You're not going to just walk away," he said. "You think I'm stupid, like Vinnie?"

"Ticky, don't call me that," Vinnie said. "I don't like it. Somebody's always saying that."

"That's because you are, Vinnie," Malone said. "You took too many punches."

Vinnie stood up, snarling. He lumbered toward Malone, pulled his switchblade and snapped it open. "I told you not to say that, Ticky." He made a lunge at Malone with the knife. Malone jumped out of the way and fired twice, striking Vinnie in the chest.

Vinnie wiped his hand across his chest and looked at the blood on it. "You killed me, Ticky." He fell to his knees, looked at Malone in disbelief, dropped the knife and collapsed to the floor.

"See what you made me do. I had to kill the dumb bastard."

"You're the one that called him stupid," I said.

Suddenly, there was a banging on the office door. "Ticky, Ticky, you in there? Open the door!" It was Sugar Lips.

Malone turned towards the door. "Yeah, everything's fine, go away."

"What was that sound? You alright?" she asked.

It was now or never. "Dawn, it's McKay. Malone's going to kill me, call the police."

Malone turned back to me, raised the revolver and squeezed the trigger. I rocked the chair over as he fired. Somehow he missed. My chair fell behind the desk. He was coming to get me. He stepped up in front of the desk and looked down at me.

"You're a hard sonofabitch to kill, McKay, I'll give you that. File or no file, you're a dead man."

I pushed my back down hard against the chair, jammed my feet against the desk and shoved as hard as I could. The desk jumped at Malone, knocking him backwards and jarring the revolver from his hand. I heard it slide across the floor. The office door swung open. It was Sugar Lips.

"The gun, get the gun, Dawn!" I shouted. 'He's going to kill us!"

Sugar Lips made a dash for the gun. Malone stuck his leg out to trip her. She stumbled over his leg and crawled on all fours toward the gun.

I could see Malone kicking at her. He connected and I heard her make a loud grunt as her hand wrapped around the gun handle. The gun barked, then again and again. I saw Malone's feet twist, then his legs fold as he came down with a crash across the top of the desk, blood squirting from his mouth and running off the desk, dripping down onto my chest and arms. He looked down at me through clouded eyes, closed them and went limp.

Sugar Lips leaned over the desk to look at Malone. She poked him with the gun barrel. "He's dead alright," I said. "You had to do it."

She was shaking. She dropped the gun and kept staring at Malone.

"Untie me," I said. She bent down and untied the knots and I shook the ropes loose, slipped the cuffs down to my feet, slipped my legs through my arms and got up.

She stumbled backwards and flopped down on the day bed. "What have I done," she said, her eyes still on Malone.

"You saved our lives, that's what you did. A second more and I would have been worm meat and you would have been next."

"I don't know," she said, a tear trickling down her cheek.

"Trust me, you did the right thing."

A few seconds later, a young uniform cop came charging through the open door, pistol in hand, a wide-eyed scared look on his face. We jumped to our feet.

"Don't shoot! It's all over, officer, watch the gun. My name's Clark McKay. Your Lieutenant Goodnight knows me." I was talking as fast as I could to get him to calm down before he shot us.

"Stay right where you are, Mister; you too, lady." He reached to his shoulder, pressed his mic button. "This is officer Dixon. Send an ambulance and back up to the Twisted Lizard. We got a shooting." He released the mic button. "Move back," he said, waving the gun at us. We backed across the floor. He bent down and checked Vinnie and Malone's pulse. "They're both dead. Sit down on the bed and stay there."

We sat down on the daybed and looked at each other. "Sorry," I said. "There was no other way."

"What now? What will they do to us?"

"I don't know."

A crowd had gathered at Malone's office door. Several young ladies were walking around topless.

"Get back from the door," the officer said, throwing up his hand in a stop motion. "Go on, get back from the door. Nobody can leave the premises until you're told to."

About twenty minutes later a plain clothes detective came in and scolded the young cop for not having the girls cover up. When the ambulance showed up the detective instructed the driver to leave the bodies where they were, and told them he would call the coroner. He spun a straight-back chair around, did a Malone and sat down backwards on the chair, unwrapped a piece of Juicy Fruit gum then stuck it in his mouth and dropped the wrapper on the floor. His jaws sagged and thick gray hair cushioned the black fedora that was pulled down over his forehead. His faded blue eyes had a far-away look, like he wanted to be somewhere else.

"My name's Detective Wallace Davenport. What's yours?" he said, looking at me.

"Name's Clark McKay."

He dropped his hands over the back of the chair and clasped his hands together, and his red striped tie did a podium swing across his pudgy stomach. "What happened here, Mr. McKay?" he asked.

"The two dead guys ran me off the road earlier this evening and kidnapped me. They would have killed me if it hadn't been for this young lady," I said, gesturing toward Sugar Lips.

He picked up speed with the gum chewing, twisted his mouth and looked at Dawn like she was an unknown species. "You're Sugar Lips Sanchez. I remember you."

"Her name's Dawn, Detective Davenport," I said. She looked at me and smiled.

"Dawn?" he said, repeating me. "Her name was Sugar Lips Sanchez when I busted her for hooking." She gave him a go to hell look and dropped her head. Davenport turned back to me. "Why would they kidnap you?"

"It gets complicated," I said.

Davenport took a pad from his coat and handed it to me with a Bic pen. "Un-complicate it," he said. "Write out a statement that makes sense while we wait for the lieutenant, it will save a lot of time." I took the pen and pad and begin to write.

Lieutenant Goodnight showed up a little later in shirt and jeans. It was three in the morning but somehow I expected him in a suit like Davenport. "What happened, McKay?" Goodnight asked.

"Malone thought I had the file, or files, that Robert supposedly took from the CIA and was going to kill me for it."

"Do you have it?"

"No."

Davenport handed Goodnight my statement and he glanced over it.

"Lieutenant," I said, "Miss Sanchez saved us both from being murdered. It's all in my statement. Could we go over it tomorrow? I'm pretty banged up."

"Yeah I can see that. You want to go to the hospital?"

"No. I just need to get out of here."

"Give me your word you will be in my office by ten in the morning and you can go home."

"You got it. What about Miss Sanchez?"

"She can go too."

"You need her to come in tomorrow," I asked.

"No, I'll wait until I hear what you have to say in the morning." He motioned for a uniform cop to take the handcuffs off. I dropped them on the bed and rubbed my sore wrist. "Wally, you stay here until the forensic guys get here. Don't let anyone else in the office. It's already contaminated," Goodnight said.

"Aren't we going to arrest them, Lieutenant?"

"No," Goodnight said.

"You believe that story?" Davenport asked, chewing his gum faster.

"Yes," Goodnight said and walked away.

Davenport shook his head and wandered off, grumbling to himself, giving the gum a workout.

"Dawn," I said. "There's something I have to know."

"Yes, I have been arrested for hooking."

"No, that's not it. I saw Malone lock the door. How did you get in?"

"Ticky always keeps a key in the cash register," she said.

"Well I'll be. Malone was a victim of his own habits. Can you make it home okay?"

"I think so," she said.

"Good. I'll talk to Goodnight in the morning. Don't worry, it will be alright."

17

got out of bed slowly and took a careful shower. My ribs were sore, my eye was swollen, and my wrist burned. When I looked in the mirror I saw this banged-up old guy that should have minded his own business, but it was too late now. I was in it up to my eyeballs, and one of them was very sore. I was way past Robert and Elle and into something I didn't bargain for...saving my own ass.

I had the routine down. The door was open. Goodnight was having his morning coffee. "Hi," he said, surprised by my sudden appearance. "You want some coffee?"

"No thanks," I said. What I really wanted was a bottle of Jack Daniels and to forget all this shit.

He looked at me and a big frown came on his face. "That eye looks worse than it did last night. What a shiner."

"Yeah. Like we say in Texas, I feel like I've been rode hard and put up wet."

"What does that mean?" he said with a puzzled look on his face.

I considered explaining and changed my mind. "Oh, nothing, you would have to know about horses."

Goodnight looked even more confused and changed the subject. "I warned you to stay out of this."

"I know, I'm a slow learner." I said.

"I read your statement again," he said. "You said Malone shot Vinnie. If Malone shot Vinnie and Miss Sanchez shot Malone with his own gun, how did she get the gun? That's the part I'm a little fuzzy on. Clear that up for me. I have to explain this to the chief."

"After Malone shot Vinnie he was trying to shoot me. I knocked the gun out of his hand by shoving the desk against him and Miss Sanchez beat Malone to the gun."

"Why did Malone want the file?" Goodnight asked.

"He said he owed a large gambling debt to the mob in Atlantic City and they would wipe it out if he got the file for them, but the guys that were collecting from him at the club worked for a local hood named Jimmy Sanfini, according to Dawn Sanchez."

"Sanfini is a part of the same family," Goodnight said. "They're all connected in one way or another."

"I'll take your word for it," I said.

"I don't think Miss Sanchez has anything to worry about," he said. "It looks like a pure case of self-defense."

"It was, nothing else," I said.

He paused, looked at me for a couple of seconds, digesting my comment.

"All right, done." He pitched the file back into the out box, took his glasses off and rubbed his chin. "Now that we

110

have that little matter done with, do you have any idea what is in that file?"

"No, but like Terrell said, it must be something important."

Goodnight shook his head. "Maybe. You going to be alright?"

"I'll make it. Did you ever find Sam?" I said.

"Not yet. Coleman either. They both disappeared about the same time. There could be a connection."

"What about the Mustang?"

"The number you gave me didn't jive with a Mustang. We're running combinations through the database. We'll find a match eventually."

"Sorry. I thought that was it. Like I told you before, I got a good memory it's just short."

Goodnight grinned. "We'll find it."

"Let me know when you do."

"Sure." He paused, clasped his hands together and began making circular motions with his thumbs. "I ran a background check on you to make sure who I was dealing with," he said. "I should have done it before now. It was impressive. I discovered you graduated at the top of your college class, married a beauty queen, had a very distinguished military career and your wife and son were killed in a car wreck by a drunk driver. I am very sorry about the loss of your family."

"Thank you. The drunk not only took the life of my wife and son, he took mine too. The only difference is I'm still breathing. All he got was a bloody nose, a fine and a suspended license. I would have killed him but I promised my dying wife I would let the courts deal with him. She was a gentle soul. Kind of ironic, considering my taste for the booze now. I'm no different than he was."

"That's not the way I see it," Goodnight said. "I know something about that. My father was an alcoholic. It killed

111

him. That doesn't have to happen to you. Don't you think it's time you call a truce with your conscience and move on before it kills you?"

"I'm trying to do that," I said.

"Don't worry about Miss Sanchez," Goodnight said. "I'll make sure this is the end of it." "Thanks," I said.

18

I left Goodnight's office and stopped off at my place to pick up the .357 and a change of clothes. I debated with myself about wearing my cowboy jacket; thought better of it and put on my funeral pants, a clean shirt, my plain leather jacket and drove to the suburbs to have dinner with Pepper.

She said Matt couldn't make it he was on duty somewhere in the Mideast.

I had just finished a great steak dinner when two cars pulled up in front of the house, turned off their lights and cut their engines.

"You see that, Colonel? That's not Matt, and I'm not expecting anyone else."

"They didn't come for dinner," I said. "Cut the lights and get down. You got a weapon?"

"A .38 in my purse. And my Berretta is in the end table by the window. It's loaded."

"Get the .38, I'll see if I can get to the window."

She stayed hunkered down, reached an arm up on the table and pulled her purse off and took the snub nosed .38 out.

"Stay down," I said and edged up to the window. I reached in the table drawer and took the Berretta out. I pulled the slide back and threw a round in the chamber. I stuck it in my belt on my back and moved beside Pepper.

It was a full moon. I saw six men get out of two cars, three ran toward the front door, the other three headed for the back. I drew the .357.

The front door slammed open, splintering the frame as the locks gave way to the force. Three men rushed in, guns drawn.

I fired twice, lighting up the room. There was a grunt and I heard a gun hit the floor as one of the men fell. Another man's silhouette appeared in the moonlight against the window. Pepper popped off two rounds and he dropped instantly without a sound. The third man suddenly leapt over the two bodies and disappeared into another room.

"I just remembered I have another gun, dad's old .45 in the bedroom. I'll get it." She jumped up and ran for the bedroom.

"No, come back." I ran after her. I ran in the bedroom behind her and a tall man dressed in black was holding a gun to her head. He had on gloves and a mask.

"Put the gun down, McKay, or I'll blow her fucking head off. You can give us the file or both die, either way we solve our problem. It's up to you."

"Who the hell are you people?" Pepper asked.

"The gun, McKay, now," he said, pushing the barrel tighter against Pepper's head.

I raised my gun slowly and tossed it in the air toward the bed. When his head snapped away from Pepper to follow the flight of the gun I grabbed the Beretta from the back of my belt and deposited a slug in his right ear hole. The other side of his head exploded with brain tissue and blood squirting out across the room like a spigot. He left a zigzag trail of blood down Pepper's body as he slid to the floor.

"You could have killed me," she said, her hand shaking as she pried the gun from the dead man's hand and picked up the .38 off the floor. "Don't you know you're a drunk?"

"You were dead for sure if I didn't shoot. It never occurred to me I could miss."

Bullets began zipping through the bedroom walls, moonlight holes appearing with every round. I saw the knob turn on the bedroom door. I picked up the .357 and put two holes chest high in the door and reloaded. The knob stopped turning. There was a thud against the door, then a voice. "I'm hit. Get the bastard."

The bedroom window shattered and I saw a hand grenade roll across the floor in the moonlight. I picked it up and threw it through the window, shattering glass everywhere. The explosion knocked us down and the world was silent for a moment.

My head was roaring. "Run," I said and pointed to the hole the grenade had blown in the wall.

"Yeah, I don't think they will renew my lease."

We made a dash for the hole in the wall, jumped through and tumbled out on the lawn and scrambled to our feet. A man and woman poked their heads out of a nearby house. "Get back inside!" I yelled and they disappeared back into the house.

A man dressed in black came flying around the corner, firing a double-tapped clipped machine pistol. Pepper

115

jumped up and emptied the dead man's automatic into him. He spun around like a windblown leaf, his finger locked on the trigger in a death grip, scattering rounds in every direction. He fell to the ground like a dropped puppet, his body sprawled in a contorted position, the pistol falling from his hand.

I saw Pepper lying on the ground, blood covering the front of her sweater. I couldn't tell how bad she was hurt. She was making a low whimpering moan. I picked her up and ran to my car, laid her on the front seat, started the engine and slammed the car in reverse.

Suddenly, a man came out of nowhere, leapt on the hood and grabbed hold with both hands. I held on to Pepper, hit the accelerator, then the brakes; his head slammed into the windshield, he lost his grip and rolled off the hood.

He wobbled to his feet and came toward me dragging one leg, jerked a weapon from his jacket, held his hand up to shield the car lights from his eyes.

I floorboarded the car. He bounced off the grill, crashed to the ground and rolled to a stop and didn't move. I spun the car around and headed for the hospital.

Five minutes later I was pulling into the emergency drive of the hospital. I quickly stashed the weapons in the hedges and carried Pepper into the emergency room. A nurse saw me, grabbed a gurney and motion for me to put her on it. Two more nurses appeared and they hauled her into a curtain-covered space as a man in a white coat rushed by me. "Wait out here," he said, waving his arm toward a row of chairs as he pulled the curtain closed.

I staggered over to a chair and sat down. A few minutes later they brought me Pepper's things in a bag.

The police showed up at the hospital not very long after. The doctor had called them when he discovered Pepper's wounds were gun shots.

An officer told me they just came from Pepper's house and I was under arrest.

"Look, officer, I shot them because they were trying to kill us. It was a home invasion. I have a right to protect myself, and my friend."

"I have to take you in. They can sort it out at headquarters. Turn around and put your hands behind your back."

"Let me keep my cell phone so I can check on her."

"I'll let you keep it till morning. I can't promise what the next shift will do."

"Let me make one phone call before you put the cuffs on me." I found Matt's number on Pepper's phone and told him what happened and that I needed him to contact a bail bondsman for me. He said he would take care of it and check on Pepper.

They put me in a cell with a ragged old wino. He saw my hands shaking and grinned. "You got it bad. How long you going to be in here?" he asked.

"I don't know."

"I get out in the morning," he said. "They usually don't keep me more than twenty-four hours. That's about as long as I can make it before I go into convulsions."

"I don't want to see that," I said.

"Me neither," he said and grinned again. "I kind of gave up on it being any other way a long time ago. I tried to go straight once. Find my family, become an upright citizen. After a week without a drink I could eat the ass out of skunk for a drink. I realized that's what I am. I'm a drunk. I'm not going to change. It looks like you're about there too."

"I'm not really in the mood for conversation." I said.

"Suits me," he said. "I can tell by the way you look at me you think you're better than I am. But you're not, you're just wearing better clothes."

I didn't know how to respond to that. I called the hospital. They said Pepper was going to be okay. She had lost a lot of blood but the bullets didn't hit any vital organs. They gave her a transfusion and a strong sedative. She would be out for a while.

I sat down on the floor with my back to the wino, pulled my knees up under my chin and clasped my hands around my legs to control the shakes. It felt like my insides were being ripped out. I got the dry heaves and my body jerked uncontrollably. The pain got so bad I passed out and went back to Vietnam, my wife was standing in front of me with blood pouring down her face. I woke up screaming.

The hopeless figure on the floor never heard me. He was in some other place twisting and jerking like a fish on a hook. He was right, I did think I was better than he was. I wasn't. I stared at the wino thinking about Mary and my boy. They would be disgusted with me if they knew what I had become. I thought about what Cleaver told me. I didn't like myself very much. For the first time in five years I didn't want a drink. I didn't know for how long, but I didn't want one now.

At 7 A.M. they brought bologna, eggs and toast for breakfast and I threw up, but nothing came out.

A couple hours later, Matt showed up and introduced himself. I think I was as embarrassed as I have ever been. He was a tall, muscular, handsome young man with bright blue eyes, blonde hair with a military haircut. He had on civilian clothes. He said they dropped the charges pending a no-bill hearing because Goodnight said we were attacked in our own domicile and were defending ourselves, but there could be some weapon charges later. I would have to say thank you to Goodnight next time I saw him.

We drove to the hospital. Matt said Pepper was still out when he left.

I called Bobby and told him what happened. "Is she going to survive?" he asked.

"She's going to be alright. She will have to stay in the hospital for a few more days. It was some mob guys, looking for a file Robert was supposed to have taken from the CIA. You ever hear your Dad mention anything about a file he had from the CIA?"

"No. Nothing I remember," he said.

"Okay, I'm going to check on Pepper, I'll call you back."

"Let me know how she's doing," he said and hung up.

I sent Matt on to Pepper's room and stopped off to get another big cup of coffee. The need for whiskey was growing. I knew now what the wino was talking about. I had an uphill battle. It was easier to accept the fact I was a drunk and give in to the urge.

As I was waiting on the elevator I overheard a nurse telling another she was treating one of the gunmen from the shooting last night in room 321.

I took the elevator up to Pepper's room. She was still out.

Matt walked over to the bed and brushed her hair away from her face.

"You going to ask her to marry you?" I asked.

"When the time is right," he said. "Colonel, I know you're a warrior, but this is not your area of expertise. I don't want Pepper killed before I get a chance to propose."

"I know this is hard for you to understand," I said, "but I have to do this and Pepper feels the same way. If you can't handle that you may have the wrong girl."

He looked at Pepper and then back to me. "Okay, what do you want me to do?"

"Keep an eye on Pepper for me for a little while. I have something I need to do."

"Sure, I'll be here," he said.

19

A young cop with his hat lying in his lap sat outside the door of room 321 reading Sports Illustrated. "That must be my boy," I said to myself.

I explored the hall and found a white lab coat in an empty office with a pair of surgical scissors sticking out of the top pocket. A nametag pinned to the pocket said 'Don Ramon, Lab Tech.' I slipped on the coat and walked out into the hall.

The cop had fallen asleep, his chair propped against the wall. He was snoring, his hat and magazine on the floor. I eased past him and quietly opened the door. The man in the bed was middle-aged, with thick curly gray hair and a fat face that needed a shave. He must have been the one behind the bedroom door.

An IV was in his arm with a heart monitor connected. He was breathing heavily in his sleep. His side and left arm were bandaged and he had a tattoo of a heart with the name Angel inside it on his right forearm.

I put on a surgical mask and an operating room hat I found in the coat along with a roll of tape. Took out the tape and taped his arms to the bed, rolled a towel up and stuck it in his mouth. His eyes popped opened. He tried to yell. I crammed more of the towel into his mouth. I threw his gown up and grabbed his balls with the scissors.

"You and me are going to have a come-to-Jesus meeting," I said, looking at his surprised face. "You make a sound I don't want you to make, I don't care if it's an oozing fart, and I'll cut your balls off and feed them to you. Do you understand? If you do, blink twice." He blinked twice so I removed the towel from his mouth.

"Who are you?" he asked.

"Now what did I just tell you, stupid?" I tightened the scissors on his balls and shoved the towel back into his mouth, he began to squirm. "You want to lose your balls?" He shook his head no. "Okay, let's try again." I pulled the towel out of his mouth. "Who sent you to kill McKay and Miss Spicier?"

"We just got a phone call. I don't know who gave the order. It could have been one of several. I didn't take the call."

I shoved the towel back in his mouth and snipped a little piece out of his balls. He let out a muffled yell. "Don't give me anymore bullshit. One more lie and I'm going to castrate you. Got it?"

He blinked his eyes twice without me telling him to. I made sure he knew I had a hold on his balls with the scissors and took the towel out of his mouth. "Who sent you?" He hesitated and I shifted my arm like I was going to cut him.

"Wait, wait," he said. "The order came from Karl Coleman."

"Where's Coleman?"

"I don't know," he said. I raised the towel to put back in his mouth. "Okay, no more cutting! He's in Reno, Nevada hiding out at the Flower Garden whore house."

"From who?"

"The cops. They got a warrant out for him."

"Who were those other scumbags with you?"

"We all work for Coleman."

"That's a good boy, now what about the file?"

"Before you start cutting, I'm telling the truth. None of us know what's in that file. We were supposed to get it from McKay." Sweat was dripping off his nose. "I'm just a soldier doing what I'm told."

"Yeah, killing people. Who killed Robert and Elle Spicier? Think before you answer." I twisted the scissors.

"Don't know, honest. Maybe it was Coleman. The house job was the only thing I was in on." I studied his face. I could see he was frightened. He was thinking of his balls.

I stuffed the towel back in his mouth, opened the door and slipped past the sleeping cop up the stairs, deposited the coat in a broom closet and went back to Pepper's room. She was still asleep and Matt was doing the same.

I tried to sleep, too, but it didn't work. The whiskey had taken its toll and my insides felt like they were on fire. I walked down to the nurses' station and got a cup of coffee and went back to Pepper's room. I was drinking the coffee when two cops walked in looking like I was going back to jail. One was big as a house with a belly to go with it. The other one was a blonde, blue-eyed kid that looked like he wasn't old enough to vote.

"You Clark McKay?" the big one asked. When he spoke he woke Matt up.

"That's me," I said.

"The hospital called us," he said. "It seems someone was in our prisoner's room last night, doing some nasty things to him."

"What's that got to do with me?"

"Come with us," the big one said. "Let's go downstairs and let the guy have a look at you."

"What you want me to do, Clark?" Matt said.

"Just stay with Pepper for now," I said.

A different cop stood outside the prisoner's door. There was no chair or magazine. We walked up to the bed and the big cop asked the wise guy if I was the one that tortured him.

"Have him say something," he said. "He was wearing a mask."

"Say something," the big cop said, nudging me closer to the bed.

"Okay…if it had been me they would have been burying your ass."

"Are you threatening the witness?" the big cop asked, wrinkling his brow.

"No, you asked me to say something. This guy tried to kill me and the girl. What do you expect me to say?"

The wise guy looked at me, then the cops and back to me, and rubbed his balls. "That's not him," he said, exhaling a deep sigh. Little beads of sweat popped out on his forehead and trickled down his cheeks. He wiped his forehead with the back of his arm and ignored the sweat on his face.

"You sure?" the big cop said.

"I'm sure. Now leave me alone," the wise guy said.

"You can go, Mr. McKay," the young cop said. The big cop turned to the young one with a surprised look. "I'll make the decisions here, Skip," the big cop said.

"Well?" I asked.

"Yeah, you can go," he said, glaring at the young cop.

20

Late that afternoon I was standing by Pepper's bed when she opened her eyes.

"Where am I?" she asked.

"You're in a hospital," I said. "You're going to be okay. You need some rest to get your strength back."

"What happened to the gunmen?"

"I punched their ticket with your help."

"All of them?"

"There's one barely kicking."

"You're a regular Wyatt Earp, Colonel. Soon as I get out of this bed we'll start kicking ass till we find out what the hell is going on. We wait on the cops we'll be dead."

I shook my head affirmative and grinned. I handed her the .38. "Might want to have this handy, just in case."

"Yeah if they run a ballistics test on those men I may have to defend myself," she said.

"Well, since you're already have a good lawyer I wouldn't worry about it," I said. She smiled and squeezed my hand.

Matt stepped up to the bed and looked at Pepper. "Hi baby."

"Matt, I'm still in a fog. I didn't see you," she said.

"You feeling any better?" he asked.

"May be a quart low and a little woozy but I'm here."

"I have to take a trip," I said.

"Where you going?" she asked, sticking the .38 under her pillow.

"To find Coleman. He's supposed to be in Reno, at a brothel called the Flower Garden."

"That should be interesting," she said.

Matt moved to the bed, sat down on the corner and took Pepper's hand. "What does this guy Coleman have to do with this, Colonel?" he asked.

"It's about the file, Matt," Pepper said "They thought we had it and was going to kill us for it. The Colonel thinks Coleman is behind it."

Matt patted Pepper's hand and looked at me. "The CIA seems to be pretty sure Mr. Spicier took the file from the archives," he said. "I can't do anything official, but if I can help in any other way let me know."

"Thanks. I would appreciate it if you would keep an eye on Pepper while I'm gone. She might need some help."

"I can do that," he said and smiled at Pepper. "Good… Pepper get well. I'll let you know if I get Coleman."

"Be careful," she said.

"I will. Talk to you when I get back," I said and walked out of the room.

I knew Pepper was in good hands so I drove to Reno. It took me three days but I needed the time to think and keep my .357. I still wasn't sure how all this tied together. What I did know for sure was Karl Coleman was responsible for the attack at Pepper's house.

Since Coleman worked for the arms company they may have a hand in this too, especially since there was a connection with Robert and Elton Parker in the CIA.

21

The Flower Garden was a large, white stucco house with a variety of flowers painted on it. A parade of men moved in and out of the house. A very large muscular black man stood inside the door directing customers to a red-carpeted waiting room to enjoy all kinds of food, drink and scantily clad women advertising their charms. When the selection was made the customer was searched by the black man before being permitted to go into a room.

A tall redhead wearing a pink see-through gown with no underwear came over and put her arm around me. She was painted up like a Mexican Ford and smelled like magnolias. She looked good, but had too many miles on the speedometer for me.

"What turns you on, honey?" she asked, running her tongue over her lips in a slow, seductive motion.

"I'm looking for a man."

"You could have fooled me."

"No, not that," I said. "I'm looking for a guy named Karl Coleman. I was told I could find him here."

"Yeah, he's here. A friend of Mickey's. He's screwing some bored housewife in room eight, hung like a horse."

"Talk about moonlighting," I said.

The redhead looked at me with a puzzled look. "Do what?" she said.

"Nothing, forget it. Who's got a key to the door?"

"You never been in a house, have you honey?"

"No, I confess. That's a part of my education I've neglected."

"We don't lock doors in a pleasure house, just set a timer. If you decide you need a little action let me know." She got up and took her place back in the meat market chorus line.

If I was going to get Coleman, now was the time. I had to get past Hercules without him searching me. What I needed was a diversionary tactic. I motioned for the redhead to come back.

"I'll give you a hundred dollars if you slap a blonde's face," I said.

"Easy money. Which one?"

"Take your pick, as long as it's a blonde. I don't like blonde women." I smiled and held up a hundred dollar bill.

"Boy, you are a strange one," she said, eyeing the bill. "Anyone of them?"

"Yeah, any of the blondes. Slap the pee out of her."

"Give me the hundred."

I tore the hundred in two and gave her half. "Here, you'll get the other half when the deed is done."

The redhead snatched the halved bill out of my hand, walked over to the smallest blonde in the room and let her have it. *Kaboom!* The blonde staggered backwards, a handprint tattooed on the side of her face.

"What are you doing, you crazy bitch!" The blonde rubbed her face and charged. The bouncer hurried to separate them.

I dropped the other half of the hundred on the floor, rushed down the hall and opened door number eight. Coleman heard the door, took a quick look over his shoulder and rolled off the bed onto the floor. A plain-looking woman about thirty drew up in a fetal position to cover her nakedness with her arms and hands.

I stuck the .357 to his head. He looked at his coat draped across a chair. "You got a gun in the coat, huh" I said. He just looked at me without expression. "Get up, or you'll be joining those assholes you sent to kill me. You, lady, get your clothes and go out that window." I pointed at a painted window with the .357.

She jumped up from the pink-covered canopy bed, grabbed her clothes and unlocked the window, raised it and climbed out naked, never saying a word.

Coleman stood up…he *was* hung like a horse.

"Can I get my clothes?" he asked.

"I'll take the coat." I snatched it off the chair and held it upside down over the bed. An automatic fell out of the pocket. "Here." I tossed him his pants then picked up the gun.

"What's this all about McKay," he said, pulling on his pants.

"Murder. And attempted murder."

"Who am I supposed to have killed?"

"Robert and Elle Spicier. And tried to kill me and Pepper Spicier."

"When was I supposed to have done that?"

"Cut the bullshit, Coleman. You may not have pulled the trigger, but you're the one that gave the order. That makes you just as guilty."

"You really think you're going to get me out of here?"

"You're going, warm or cold. I don't care which."

"I'm going to tear your head off is what I'm going to do. Old man."

"Yeah, I see how brave you are; hiding in a whore house, playing patty cake with

desperate women."

I heard a noise behind me, then a voice.

"Drop the gun, Clark." It was Sam. "Drop it," he said again. "Put the gun on the floor slowly and turn around."

"He's got my gun in his belt, Sam," Coleman said.

"That one too, Clark," Sam said.

I knew Sam hit what he aimed at. I bent down and placed the guns on the floor and turned around. Sam Had a Glock with a silencer trained on me.

Coleman picked up the guns, grabbed his shirt and threw it over the camera. "Let me kill this cocksucker, Sam, before he causes anymore trouble."

"Not yet. How did you know where to find us, Clark?"

"One of Colman's cronies has a big mouth."

"No matter, we were coming after you anyway. Now we don't have to."

"I figured that, thought I would beat you to the punch. You set me up at the cabin and all those questions about Robert, taking the Lincoln to search. You knew the car the train ran over was a Mercedes. No one told you. It all added up, I just didn't want to believe it. My two best friends turned out to be my worst nightmare."

"We like money, Clark. We sure as hell weren't going to get much working for the government. Unfortunately, Robert made some bad decisions. Where's the file?"

"I don't have the file, Sam, never did."

"Clark, to put it in terms you understand, this is not my first rodeo. You know I've checked you out. Robert registered a package at the post office addressed to you ten days before he met his untimely death. He had a signed receipt from you in his wallet."

"That was a framed picture of me, you and Robert on our last day in Nam, when we were waiting for our flight back home during a monsoon. Now I have to throw it away."

"Oh, that breaks my heart," Sam said, mocking me. "I could give a shit less. I never did like taking orders from you anyway. Now I give the orders. The old man said get the file so I'm going to get the file."

"Who's the old man?"

"You don't need to know. Give me the file, Clark."

"I'm a little confused, Sam. People keep trying to kill me. How can I give you the file if I am dead?"

"Good question, Clark. You see, we figure you're the only one that knows where it is. So either way it's over, although it would be better to have the file just to make sure. The choice is up to you."

"I think I would have to agree with that last part," I said.

"Let me have him for five minutes and he'll cuss his mother when I get through with him," Coleman said.

"Like I said, I give the orders. Shut up Coleman."

"I don't have the file, Sam. I don't even know what's in it. If you're going to kill me do it. It doesn't matter anymore."

Sam studied me for a second or two and sighed. "He doesn't have the file, Karl. I know him. He's not lying."

"Well if he doesn't have it, who does?" Coleman said.

"No one, Robert hid it. We have to find out where. The old man's going to be pissed off like a Russian bear, but Clark doesn't have it."

There was a tap on the door. A sultry woman's voice asked, "Are you through with the room?"

"Go away. I'll let you know when I'm through," Coleman said.

"We got to figure out how we want to do this." Sam said. "Go get Mickey, Karl."

"Okay, but I've got it figured out. I'll fuck Mickey and shoot the sonofabitch. How's that?" Coleman said and laughed.

"That's it, you just bought a one-way ticket to hell," Sam said. The Glock made a muffled puff sound as Sam put a bullet between Coleman's eyes.

Coleman never uttered a word, just crashed to the floor facedown with a thud like a chopped-down tree, a blood puddle around him on the shiny hardwood floor.

Sam walked over and kicked his dead body. "I told you, one more shitty remark about Mickey and I was going to kill your ass. You didn't listen."

"Looks like I don't have to worry about him anymore," I said. "How are you going to explain killing him?"

"There's a warrant for him," Sam said. "Found him in a whorehouse, he resisted arrest, I had to shoot. You, I figure Lake Tahoe."

Someone banged on the door, and the voice was back. "Mickey says to stop the noise and get out of the room now. We got other customers."

"Who's Mickey, Sam?"

"My sister. She owns the house. Now you know why I never talked about family. The only family I had was a whore. Like they say, old whores never die they just turn into madams." Sam showed a faint smile that quickly faded.

He held the gun on me with one hand and reached in his shirt pocket with the other and took out a Marlboro pack. He shook a cigarette halfway out of the pack, brought it straight to his mouth. He tossed the pack on a table, pulled a lighter out of his pants pocket, set fire to the cigarette, took a deep drag. A pleased expression appeared as he exhaled.

"Clark, I feel bad it has come to this, but you're a liability I can't afford." Sam raised the gun toward me. "There's some Jack Daniels in the cabinet. I can at least let you have a last drink."

"I quit," I said.

"Sure you did. Suit yourself, time's up."

In the next instant the door flew open. The big black guy stepped inside. "What the hell," he said, looking at Coleman then Sam. "What are you doing in here Sam? What happened to him?"

Sam turned to him, letting the gun drop to his side. "Close the damn door, Ellis!"

In the next instant, Pepper appeared at the open window. "Colonel, the window," she said and stuck her .38 through the open window, firing at Sam. She missed and Sam dropped down behind the bed. I scooped up the .357 as I ran across the room, dove out the open window and came up running, fishing for my keys. Pepper was close behind. I found the keys and we jumped in the car.

"What you doing here? You're supposed to be in the hospital," I said as I stabbed at the ignition slot with the keys.

"Thought I would apply for a job."

"You're crazy as I am, girl." I fired up the engine and hauled ass. Sam was running toward the car, raising his gun to fire as I peeled out of the parking lot.

"You could have gotten killed back there, Pepper."

"What do you think Sam was going to do to you? Play chess?"

"Yeah, you showed up in the nick of time as usual. You got a car here?"

"No I flew, took a taxi," she said.

"I may have to put you in my will."

"I thought I already was?"

"You are." We both laughed and headed for the capital.

22

After getting Pepper settled into a new place my first stop was to see if the Twisted Lizard was open. A sign nailed to a post said it would reopen Saturday. Today was Friday. It was my guess that whoever was running the Lizard would have a connection to Malone's gambling buddies and they would lead me to the people who wanted that file so damn bad, and I would make them pay for it.

I decided to pay a visit to Sugar Lips to see if she had some names for me. Her car wasn't there. I pulled in the drive way to turn around and noticed the glass in the front door was shattered and the door not completely closed. I cut the engine off, got out and took a closer look. As I stepped inside the door, a stench I was familiar with attacked me. The smell was much stronger than dirty dishes this time. It was the smell of death.

I drew the .357 and moved slowly through the house. I opened the kitchen door and almost stepped on a knife. Utensils were scattered around on the floor. I walked down a short hallway to a bedroom; opened the bedroom door, carefully pushing it open wider with the pistol. Lying on the unmade bed was the naked body of Dawn "Sugar Lips" Sanchez. A butcher knife stuck between those perfect breasts covered in dried blood. There were several cuts on her arms. She must have tried to fight off her attacker. She was barely recognizable. Her eyes were half open with a milky-colored cloud over them. Her decomposing body had turned purple.

She had something clutched in her right hand. Her long pink nails were broken on both hands. I pried open her hand and a lock of black hair fell out. The hair was coarse and oily. Her hair was fine and shiny. I rubbed it in my hand and some of the black came off on my fingers. Whoever the hair belonged to had dyed it. I put the hair back in her hand and forced her hand closed.

Torn red panties were lying on the floor. A stack of crumpled up bills - ones, fives, tens and twenties - were on her bedroom dresser. I checked her answering machine and there were no messages. I knew I would catch hell from Goodnight, but I closed her eyes and pulled a sheet over her. I checked her bathroom for hair dye. There was none.

I called Goodnight, told him what I found and gave him the address. I left out the part about the hair dye. I should have told him what happened to Coleman too, but I decided against it. I had a personal score to settle with Sam and Coleman was probably in Lake Tahoe.

Goodnight said to wait outside until he got there and not to touch anything. It was too late for that. I stuck the .357 in the spare tire hole and waited.

Goodnight and Davenport showed up about an hour later, with a coroner ambulance and doctor right behind them.

"Why do people turn up dead everywhere you go, McKay?" Davenport said.

"I don't need your kind of shit, Detective. You want to be next?"

"Hey, both of you take it easy," Goodnight said. "Cool off. Let's take a look at the body."

"It's in the bedroom," I said.

A man in a white coat handed us masks and we walked back to the bedroom.

Goodnight noticed the sheet over Dawn. "Did you find her that way?"

"No. I felt like I should do something for her."

"I thought so," Goodnight said. "Did you touch the knife?"

"No."

"That's good. If your prints were on the murder weapon it could complicate things," Goodnight said.

"Yeah, you could be a suspect," Davenport said.

"If I killed her why would I come back here and call you?"

"Murderers have done dumber things," Davenport said.

I ignored Davenport's comment. He was deliberately trying to piss me off. "I don't think Dawn had any family. Let me know when I can bury her and I'll pay for the funeral."

"Feeling guilty, McKay?" Davenport said.

"That's enough, Wally." Goodnight said.

"I'll wait outside." Davenport gave me a snarl, unwrapped a piece of Juicy Fruit gum and stuck it in his mouth, gave his fedora a tug and walked away.

"Can I go?" I asked.

"Yes, go on. I'll let you know if I need you," Goodnight said. "By the way, we haven't turned up anything on Sam or Coleman yet."

"You may not," I said.

"Why's that?"

"Don't know. Just got a feeling," I said.

I left Goodnight and Davenport to their investigation and drove away. It was good to get some fresh air. I had a sinking feeling in the pit of my stomach and thought I would throw up. I knew Sugar Lips' murder and that damn file had something to do with it. I understood where she was coming from. She had to survive and did it the only way she knew how.

When I got to my room I headed straight for the bathroom, peeled off my clothes and turned the water on as hot as I could stand it. I stood there watching the steam rise from the floor, thinking about Dawn. I failed her. I didn't know exactly how, I just did. It took a while to wash the smell of death away. The memory of it never leaves.

23

The next morning I got dressed, made coffee and called Pepper. "You okay kid?"

"Yeah, how about you?" she said.

"I'll live...I need a favor."

"You got it."

"See if you can find out anything from the DC police lab about a Dawn Sanchez, better known as Sugar Lips. I found her dead yesterday. She's been trying to help us unravel your parents' murder. I'm pretty sure the police took some evidence to the police lab that might tell us who did it. I need to know what they found."

"Sorry to hear that, Colonel. I remember you talking about her. I'll let you know if he comes up with anything."

"Thanks," I said and hung up.

When I walked in the Twisted Lizard that night a pretty young blonde with over-sized tits was working the crowd. Several men at different tables were calling for Sugar Lips. The call of "We Want Sugar Lips" became louder and louder, with more men joining in until the blonde ran off stage crying. A man came on stage and announced that Sugar Lips would not be back. He said it like he knew what I knew. The noise subsided and the young blonde finished her act without much applause or money.

The man that made the announcement walked around talking to customers and employees. It was obvious he was in charge. I had never seen him before. He was about six feet, over forty with slick-down black hair combed straight back and a short well-trimmed black beard. He wore a black pinstriped suit over his bulky frame with a hunter green turtleneck sweater and a large diamond ring on his right hand.

Three other men that looked like bouncers walked around the room checking IDs and quieting down troublemakers.

I found an empty two-chair table at the back of the room and sat down. After a few minutes one of the topless waitresses jiggled over to me to take my order. The guy at the next table ordered a Coors Light so I did too, although I had no intention of drinking it.

When she came back with the beer I asked who the guy in the suit was. She said his name was Wendell Overa. He was the new manager. I remembered the young cop at the hospital saying he was the one who rented the Mercedes. I wondered why he wasn't in jail. He walked past me without paying any attention to me or saying anything. He picked up a stack of money at the bar and made his way between the tables to the office, nodded to the bouncer stationed at the door and went in.

My phone rang. It was Pepper. "Matt called. He said his friend with the police said they had a match with an ex-con named Wendell Overa that they found in their database. The semen and the hair had his DNA on it. They're keeping it quiet until they can get a judge to issue an arrest warrant tomorrow. Matt said to remind you to not reveal where you got the info."

"Thanks Pepper. Tell Matt I owe him one."

"You bet," she said. If Overa found out about the warrant he would be long gone. I wasn't going to let that happen.

I hung up, left a twenty on the table and walked over to the bouncer at the office door. He looked like he could be Vinnie's bother. "I need to see Mr. Overa," I said.

"What about?" the man asked.

"It's personal. He's expecting me."

"Yeah? Let me ask him."

As he turned toward the door I ran the barrel of my gun between his legs. "Walk on in real quiet-like. One sound and I'll make you a new asshole."

I reached inside his coat and removed an automatic from his shoulder holster. I pushed him up against the door, he opened it. I shadowed him in. Overa was sitting at Malone's desk counting money. Everything looked the same, including the bullet holes in the wall.

"Who's this Tommy?" Overa asked, gesturing toward me.

"I don't know. He said he was here to see you and jammed a pistol up my ass."

"Put your gun on the desk real slow, Overa," I said.

He hesitated for a moment so I cocked the hammer on the .357 and he stood up and laid a Glock on the desk. "You don't need a gun, mister," he said. "Take the money. You won't live to spend it, but take it."

"I don't want your money. I want the lowlife that raped and killed Dawn Sanchez."

143

"I don't know anything about that," Overa said. "She called in the other day saying she quit, didn't want to work for me. That's all I know."

"You knew she was dead though?"

"Yeah, I heard that from somebody."

The bouncer made a step toward me. "Don't do it numb nuts," I said and he stepped back. "Take off your shoes and socks," I said to the pug.

"What for?" he asked.

"Just do it. And hand me the socks." He did as I told him and handed me the socks. "Sit down," I said and slid a chair under him. He sat down and I jerked the phone cord out of the wall and tied his hands behind his back to the chair and stuffed his socks in his mouth. A sick expression appeared on his face. "It's your feet," I said. "Alright Overa, now that I have your friend properly gift wrapped come here."

He stared at me and didn't move. "Come here, before I shoot your ass." He took three steps toward me and stopped. I placed the gun against his head and ran my fingers through his hair. Black dye came off on my hand.

"What're you doing, you faggot," he said, jerking his head back.

"You're the one. You raped and murdered Dawn." I tightened my finger on the trigger. It was all I could do to keep from blowing him away.

"Now I know who you are," Overa said. "You're that McKay guy that got Malone killed by that whore. There's a dozen more right outside the door." He pointed at the door. "Go pick you one. My treat."

"Why did you have to kill her?" I asked.

"I didn't. You got the wrong guy."

"I don't think so, you left a calling card," I said, holding up the palm of my hand for him to see the black dye.

"You're making a mistake. I work for the family."

"I don't have a family, so I don't give a shit. Open the back door."

Overa unlocked the door. I shoved him through the open door into the parking lot. Every time he slowed his pace I nudged him with the gun. I told him to get in the driver's seat and I got in the back.

"I hope you can drive," I said. I reached around him, stuck the keys in the ignition and started the car. "Okay let's go."

"Go where?"

"Drive. I'll tell you as we go."

I called Goodnight's home number and let it ring until he answered.

"This better be important," he said.

"It is. I got a present for you."

"What?" he asked.

"Do you know what time it is?"

"Yeah, it's a little after two A.M. What do you want, McKay?"

"I got the guy that killed Dawn Sanchez."

"I told you I didn't do it," Overa said.

"Who was that?" Goodnight asked.

"That's him. I'm bringing him in on a citizen's arrest."

"Are you sure he's the one?"

"Your lab found some dyed black hair and semen that matches."

"You know more than I do. I know the lab was checking but they haven't told me anything."

"Well they told me."

"What?"

"Never mind. Get up and meet me at the station before this guy's buddies discover he's gone."

"You're absolutely sure?"

"I am." I walked him into the police station with my hand in my jacket. He didn't know I left the gun in the car.

145

Overa kept insisting he knew nothing about Dawn's murder, telling Goodnight I kidnapped him, threatened to shoot him, and he was going to sue for false arrest and wanted to call his lawyer.

"You better be right, McKay. I've stuck my neck way out on a limb. I can hold him for twenty-four hours. If we don't have some hard evidence by then we're going to be in a world of hurt."

"He's the one. Check with your lab in the morning. I'm sure it's a match."

"How do you know that?"

"A little birdie told me."

"We may need your little birdie to sing for a judge if we can't find anything on this guy."

"You will. Call me."

The next morning around nine thirty Goodnight called. "You were right, McKay. It was a match," he said. "The blood, semen and hair were all matches. We should have a complete DNA report in a few days, but it looks like Overa's our man."

"Sometimes it's better to be lucky than good."

"What! You put my ass on the line and you were guessing?"

"Time to go, see you," I said and hung up.

The next day I cleared it with a still upset Goodnight to have the funeral for Dawn.

"I'll have the funeral home pick her up and bury her," I said.

"Okay if I show up?" Goodnight asked.

"Sure. Thanks, I appreciate that."

The funeral home had her ready the next day. I stopped by, paid them and we drove out to the graveyard for a graveside ceremony in drizzling rain. I was pretty sure she was Catholic. I saw a rosary on her bedroom dresser. I arranged for a priest to meet us at the graveyard. To my surprise Pepper was there.

"You didn't have to come, Pepper, but I'm glad you did," I said.

"I knew this would be hard on you. I didn't know her but she gave her life trying to help us. This is the least I can do."

Goodnight drove up as the hearse driver and his helpers were unloading the casket. The wet red clay walls of the grave were slick and shiny, like strawberry icing on a cake. I could see my shimmering reflection looking back at me on the shiny wet casket as they carried it to the grave. My thoughts turned to Mary and Cooper. Sometimes the pain was almost unbearable.

The priest read several passages from the Bible, including John 3:16, and asked the Lord to take this poor soul into heaven. He said Ah-men and walked away.

I gave the okay and they lowered the casket into the grave. I tossed a white rose into the grave and told the grave diggers to close it up.

Goodnight said he was sorry about Dawn, but at least we had the man that killed her. That was some conciliation for us, but it didn't do Dawn any damn good. Some people are just born under the wrong star, at the wrong time, in the wrong place. We both had our demons. Maybe that was why I could understand about hers. It's easy for someone that doesn't have them to tell you how to get rid of them, but only someone that has them can really know the torment and how hard it is to let them go. I was finding that out firsthand every day.

I would tell myself one little drink won't hurt. But if there was one, I knew there would be a dozen or more to follow.

24

After the funeral I drove back to my motel. I pulled up to my room and noticed the gum wrapper I stuck in the door was gone. I stepped out of the car, drew the .357 and crept carefully along the wall to the edge of the window. I heard a sound behind me.

Before I could turn to the sound someone clobbered me from behind. My knees buckled and I went down and dropped the gun. Someone was dragging me by the arms through the doorway. They were talking but I couldn't understand the words. My head was spinning, everything was on a merry-go-round. Through the fog I saw a man with a big bent nose. It was like having a sign hanging around his neck that read 'Sanfini.' They threw me across the bed and handed Sanfini the gun. The merry-go-round began to slow down and I could see better.

A big, ugly-looking brute with a severe case of acne stood silent in the corner with a nine-millimeter machine pistol pointed at me. A tall, thin man moved back and forth behind me with a .45 pointed at me on the other side of the bed.

Sanfini sat down, took a big drag on his cigar, leaned forward and blew smoke in my face. "Listen to me McKay," he said, "I want the file and I want it now. My boss said I have to come up with it. That means you're going to tell me where it is."

"What part of 'no' don't you idiots understand? I don't have the file, for the umpteenth time."

"Ace, come here," Sanfini said.

"Yeah boss."

"You got your knife?"

"Yeah boss."

"Cut off McKay's little finger. Maybe that will show him we mean business."

The thin man flipped open a switchblade, grabbed my right arm and slammed my hand down on the table. I pulled away, but the brute in the corner ran over and put a choke hold on me while Sanfini held the other arm.

Ace brought the knife down hard, cutting off my little finger below the first joint. I screamed and blood gushed out, pushing the amputated finger across the table until it tumbled off onto Sanfini's mirror-shined shoes.

Sanfini looked down at his shoes, shook his foot and the bloody finger rolled off onto the floor. "You're bleeding all over the place." He jerked a handkerchief out of his pocket, reached down and wiped the blood off his shoes and threw the handkerchief on the floor. "Get him a towel, Ace, he's bleeding like a stuck hog."

Sanfini pulled out a new cigar and lit it with an old Zippo lighter and sat down on the corner of the bed. "You see this lighter," he said, holding it up to my face.

I was drifting in and out of consciousness.

"Belonged to my old man," he said. "He was in the Army too. World War II, the big one. Only thing he left me." He looked at the lighter and sighed. "My old man was a sonofabitch. Would whip my ass at the drop of a hat." He flipped the top up, stuck his thumb on the lighter wheel and spun it. A flickering flame jumped up and danced across the top of the lighter. A broad smile came across his face. He snatched the towel from my finger, grabbed my hand and stuck the flame to the end of my severed finger I let out a yell and jerked my hand away. He closed the lighter top and laughed.

"That should stop the bleeding." He tossed the lighter up in the air, caught it and stuck it back in his pocket, a smile on his face. "We wouldn't want you to bleed to death before you tell us where that file is. My boss would be very unhappy."

Ace began to laugh and they all joined in. I concentrated on my anger for Sanfini to help control the pain

Sanfini sat in the chair. The thin man stood beside the chair with his knife in his hand. The brute leaned against the motel door cradling the machine pistol. I had been in some jams before but this may be the worst, including Vietnam.

"Why do you want to be so stubborn?" Sanfini said. "You wouldn't be in this predicament if you had turned the file over to start with. Now you're going to get cut up into little pieces for nothing. Tell you what…you tell me where the file is and we won't cut you up. If you don't, well, I think you know what will happen. Ace gets to make a pin cushion out of you."

"All you dumbasses want to do is carve people up. It won't matter what you do to me, I don't have or even know where the file is."

"You know we don't believe that, McKay, or we wouldn't be here. You're beginning to be a real pain in the ass."

"You kill Robert and Elle Spicier?" I asked.

"Won't do any good to try and change the subject but no, I didn't do it."

"But you know who did."

"Maybe."

"What difference is it going to make if you tell me, you're going to kill me anyway."

"That's true," he said, a big smile creeping across his face. "You're good as dead but I wouldn't feel right about it. You know, honor among thieves and that kind of stuff." They all laughed again. "Enough talking, McKay. Ace, it's time to work on the other pinkie."

Ace got a grip on his knife and started toward me. The sound of running feet from outside the motel room got everyone's attention.

"What was that?" Sanfini said.

A magnified voice from outside the motel yelled, "Police, open up!"

All three men looked at each other surprised.

"Ask them what they want McKay," Sanfini whispered. "Nothing else." Sanfini stuck the gun in my back. "Do it or I'll kill you now," he said in a calm, low voice.

"What's the problem, officer?" I said loud enough to carry outside.

"The clerk called us, said he heard someone screaming in the room. Open up."

"That was the TV. I was watching a war movie, Lieutenant Goodnight. It's pretty good." I hoped to hell Sanfini didn't know who Goodnight was. We waited in silence for several seconds.

Suddenly the motel window exploded, propelling pieces of glass across the room. Everyone in the room ducked. Two officers rammed open the door and rushed in, weapons drawn. I backed up against the wall with my hands up. Sanfini fired, hitting the first man through the door in the face and he fell dead in the doorway, a red sheet of blood covering his face. The other officer quickly returned fire, streaking Sanfini in his neck and nose. Sanfini dropped his gun, grabbed his face with both hands and staggered back against the wall and fell to the floor on his back, blood spurting up like a fountain from where his nose used to be

The one Sanfini called Ace ran in the bathroom and locked the door. The brute dropped his machine pistol. "Don't shoot! I give up," he said, cowering in the corner.

"I'm not armed," I said, holding my hands in the air. Another officer came through the door. It was Corporal Dixon.

"Don't shoot," he said, "I know this man. Mr. McKay get outside."

I dropped my hands and hurried outside.

The cop standing beside me saw my finger. "Man what happened?"

"It wasn't a shaving accident."

"You going to be alright?" he asked.

"I think so. I'm a little woozy, but thanks to one of those pricks you blew away in there the bleeding stopped."

"You need to go to the hospital?"

"I could use a bandage if you have a first aid kit." "Yeah, I got one in the cruiser."

He returned with the bandage and I wrapped my finger and sat down beside one of the squad cars, fighting to stay conscious.

Corporal Dixon stood beside the bathroom door pleading for the man to come out. Ace fired four shot through the door. Dixon stood tight against the wall. He reached around with his weapon arm and fired several shots into the bathroom door. A few seconds later blood ran out from under the door and streamed down the edge of the tile to the carpet.

Dixon motioned for one of the other cops. They counted "one, two, three" and threw their shoulders against the door, bursting the lock and cracking the door wide enough to see Ace lying on the floor.

Dixon came walking out, holding his revolver by his side. "I tried to get him to come out," he said.

My head was full of mixed emotions; of anger, relief and just plain glad to be alive. The glad to be alive part surprised me. Maybe I did want to live.

"Corporal, this is twice you have saved my bacon. Thank goodness Sanfini didn't know who Goodnight was."

"You're lucky it was me. When you said you were watching a movie about Lieutenant Goodnight it took me a minute to put it together. How do you keep getting in these situations?"

"Just lucky I guess."

"You sure you don't need to go to the hospital? You should have some stitches in that finger."

"I'll be alright once I get away from here."

Dixon nodded. "Alright, if the Lieutenant can trust you I can too. Come by the station before ten in the morning and we will sort all this out. I have to file a report for Lieutenant Goodnight."

"Thanks, I'll be there. I'll get my stuff."

I walked back into the room. My gun had been kicked under the edge of the bed. I bent over and quickly slipped it in my bag and gathered up my things.

Then I watched the ambulance load up what was left of Sanfini and Ace. I waved goodbye to Dixon, threw the bag in the car, got in and headed for parts unknown.

People kept trying to kill me over something I didn't have and didn't have a clue where it was. My finger hurt like hell but it wasn't all bad. It looked like I had literally dodged a bullet, again. Time to find a new home. I was definitely a rolling stone. I moved more than Mayflower.

25

I found a room for rent that afternoon in a retired auditor's house with a private entrance. I had trouble sleeping – got up before dawn the next morning, re-taped my finger, threw down a handful of Tylenol. On my way to the police station I slowed down twice when I saw liquor stores, but somehow found the resolve to drive on to the station. Corporal Dixon was satisfied with my explanation and said he would turn his report over to Goodnight.

It was almost noon by the time I got out of the police station. I was getting hungry and remembered a greasy spoon café where I could indulge myself in forbidden food and try to make sense of all this cloak and dagger stuff.

Landry's Café was not on the Washington five-star dinning list but they did have the best hamburgers in town. Piles of onions, tomatoes, cheese and lettuce, with an inch-thick broiled patty simmered in a special secret sauce…man, that's living.

The café was no more than twenty-five-feet wide and forty-feet long, with a bright blue countertop on a counter that ran the length of the room. Salt and pepper shakers, napkin holders and toothpick jars sat on the counter directly across from each stool. Eight booths lined the other wall. Bad paintings of all the presidents, from George to George, hung on the wall next to the booths. They hadn't gotten around to Obama yet. Customers had scribbled uncomplimentary remarks on several of them. Some of the comments had been marked out.

I walked past an elderly lady dipping a tea bag in a cup and then squeezed by a fat man with a large plate of fries and two Hamburgers. Two homeless-looking men with long dirty hair and beards, wearing thread-worn army field jackets and fatigue pants, sat in the next-to-last booth pouring something from a paper bag into their coffee cups. I sat down in the last booth with my back against the wall.

An old, rail-thin black man wearing a net over his white kinky hair, an apron and thick glasses, moved hamburgers around on the grill with his spectacle-like checkers. He gave a wave to everyone that came in but never said a word. It was rumored he was once a chef at the White House.

A plump, middle-aged waitress chewing gum and wearing a bad-looking black wig brought me a cup of coffee. I didn't order it, but they always brought you a cup and you paid a buck fifty whether you drank it or not. Most people didn't drink it. There was a sneaking suspicion by the regulars that they poured what was left in your cup back in the pot and served it again.

"Bring me a hamburger special with everything," I said. The waitress nodded, wrote my order on her pad and left.

My cell rang, it was Goodnight. "You okay?" he asked.

"I'll live. What's going on. Lieutenant?"

"Dixon told me about Sanfini and your finger"

"Was that why you called me? You were concerned about my welfare?"

"That was part of it. I have something else." He paused. "I wanted to tell you that Wendell Overa wants to strike a plea. He can help us nail some of the big boys we've been trying to get. Before I talk to the D.A., I wanted you to know."

"Well, if he's willing to confess, and you think you have him anyway, why not give him the needle. And while you're at it, ask him if he knows where that CIA file is." I said.

"He won't talk without a deal."

"Have you considered torture?"

"You got a weird sense of humor, McKay."

"I didn't mean for it to be funny. I want that bastard dead."

"The thing is, I think the D.A. will want to take the deal to clear a lot of cases without spending taxpayer money. It's an election year."

"Oh that's different, we certainly want him to be reelected," I said sarcastically. "Everything's politics. If you've already made your decision why are you telling me?"

"He also said he could tell us who murdered the Spiciers. If he can, the case is solved, you can go home. It's over."

"What about the file?"

"What about it? If there is such a thing, let the CIA and FBI handle it. You need to let it go. If we find out who killed the Spiciers that should end it for you."

"Yeah, you're right," I said. I knew there was no reason to discuss it any further. Overa would lie and I would have to find the file on my own. Besides, it wasn't like I had a family to go home to.

The waitress came with my pound of hamburger, logger fries and a bottle of catsup. I was in obese heaven.

I ate every bite and walked out of the greasy spoon, waiting for indigestion to set in when I saw a for sale sign on a '73 Chevy Super Sport with those classic twin stripes parked across the street. There were 454 horses waiting for someone to say "giddy up!" I walked over to get a closer look and called the number on the sign.

A forty-plus black man showed up wearing a navy blue pea coat, jeans, a number twenty-three Redskins jersey and a suspicious look.

I checked under the hood. No oil leaks, nothing loose. I owned one I bought new in '73 for thirty-five-hundred. Reconditioned, this one would be worth ten times that now. I took it for a spin and we haggled over the price and settled on eight thousand. I had the money wired to his bank. He signed the title over to me. I put it in the glove box. I would register it later. I called the rental company to come pick up their car.

I swung by my old motel in my new, but old, car to thank the clerk that saved me from Sanfini.

"Hi," I said. "Thanks for calling the cops. Your name's Sidney, right?"

"Sidney Blankenship," he said, removing his Yankees baseball cap. He had cocker spaniel eyes, a humble smile and his thin frame made you want to feed him.

"Sidney, you're my hero."

He blushed and gave me that ah shucks smile again. "You're welcome," he said, putting his cap back on. "I'm sorry for letting them in your room. They said they were the police. One of them showed me a badge."

"A badge? You mean a police badge?"

"I thought I was doing the right thing."

"Was the guy that showed you the badge in uniform?"

"No. He had on a suit and wore one of those forties-type felt hats with the brim turned down in front. You know, like you see in the old Humphrey Bogart movies."

"A fedora?"

"Whatever you call them," he said.

"You remember his name?"

"I think it was Porter. Portman? Something like that. The police asked me the same question. I couldn't remember."

Then it hit me. "How about Davenport?"

"That was it," he said, pushing his baseball cap back on his head, his eyes lighting up.

"You sure?"

"I am now. That was it, Davenport. I remember now. I'm sure."

"Would you testify to that in court?"

"I don't know about that. I'm sure it was Davenport, but I got my family to think of Mr. McKay."

"I understand. That's okay Sidney. Thanks again," I said.

I climbed back in the Super Sport and drove away. I hoped nothing happened to the little fellow. I owed him big time.

Part 3
Who Did It

26

I stopped at a convenience store and checked the phonebook for Davenport's address. He wasn't listed. I called the electric company using my best New England accent.

"My name is Wallace Davenport." I said. "I have not received a bill in two months. I have had to call your office for my bill the last two months and I am very upset about it. You must have the wrong address. What address do you have?"

"12180 India Drive, Washington D.C. That's right, isn't it Mr. Davenport?" the voice asked.

"Um, yeah, that's right. Forget it. I'll probably get a bill next month," I said and hung up. Davenport was telling me about criminals doing stupid things and he gives the motel clerk his real name. Talk about stupid. I looked up the address on a local map.

The house was a moderate two-story brick on a quiet street. There wasn't a car in the driveway but the garage door was closed, there could be one in there.

I parked down the street, decided to live dangerously, and walked back to the house and took a quick peek in the garage window. I froze in my tracks. There it was, a black Mustang with Virginia plates. I would bet a hundred to one the brakes squeaked.

I called Goodnight and asked him to meet me at Landry's Café at three. I had information about a dirty cop and thought we should discuss it in private. He agreed.

The Super Sport was my little secret, so I parked a couple of blocks away and walked to the café. I stood inside, looking out the big plate glass window, waiting for Goodnight.

Goodnight arrived shortly after I did, parked his car in a no parking zone and hurried in. I motioned for Goodnight to follow me to my favorite booth. The same waitress that waited on me before brought two cups of coffee, whipped out her order pad and looked at Goodnight.

"I didn't order coffee," Goodnight said.

"It's alright, it's on me Lieutenant." I turned to the waitress. "Nothing else."

She stopped chewing her gum, held her order pad between two fingers and dropped it into her apron pocket from a foot above it. "What do you think this is a rest stop?" she said and strolled away.

"What's her problem?" Goodnight asked, watching her walk away.

"Forget it," I said.

"I thought we agreed this was over for you and you were going home."

"I was, then this happened. There has to be a connection to Robert and Elle's murders."

"Alright. I don't have much time, get on with it."

"What if I told you that Mr. Morgan was right about the Mustang. I know where the car is, and the guy that has it is your own Detective Wallace Davenport. Not only that, but the clerk at the motel said Davenport showed him his badge and let Sanfin in my room. How about them apples?"

"Are you out of your mind? Wallace Davenport has been on the force for twenty-five years and has a boat load of medals. I know you two don't hit it off, but of all people on the force he would be the last one I would suspect."

"Exactly, that's why he's been able to get away with it."

"How do you know Davenport has a Mustang?"

"I peeked in his garage window and there it was, a black Mustang just like the one that was following me. Here's the tag number," I said, handing him the number. "This time it's the right number. Check it out."

"Okay, I'll check on it. You stay away from Davenport's house and let me find out what's going on."

"Yeah, okay. Just do it soon before something happens to the Mustang."

"I will." He looked down at my finger. "You better see a doctor about that finger, there's blood coming through the bandage."

"It's alright." I said, covering it with my other hand.

Goodnight pitched a five on the table, got up and left.

In spite of Goodnight's warning, I went back to Davenport's house and parked at the end of the street where I could see him coming. After a couple of hours, a black Ford Victoria sedan with an antenna on the trunk pulled into his drive way. The car was unmarked but the model and antenna said police car.

Davenport and a younger man, a little taller, with short black hair, got out of the Sedan. The younger man had a badge and a snub-nosed .38 in a holster on his belt, with a leather jacket draped over his arm and carrying a big bucket of KFC. Davenport was wearing his trademark Fedora, carrying a brief case. Davenport looked my way and I slid down in the seat. They went in the house. I ate my peanut butter crackers and waited.

Later they came out, opened the garage door, got in the Mustang, and drove out the other end of the street. I followed for several miles through some of the more seedy areas. We crossed the Anacostia River. Garbage and a variety of other discarded waste floated by. We were definitely on the wrong side of town. This was the kind of place that the cops went in armed to the teeth any time they had a call.

About three miles from the river, the Mustang pulled into a blind alley and stopped beside a red steel cargo door. Davenport put his cell phone up to his ear and shortly afterward two black men wearing sweats with hoods came out of the door with a briefcase. Davenport's partner got out of the Mustang and gave the two men another briefcase. They opened it on the trunk of the car and nodded yes to him and handed him their briefcase.

A dirty old man staggered into the alley with his hand out, begging the men for money. One of the black men shoved the old man to the ground and they both disappeared behind the red cargo door. The man with Davenport pitched some change on the ground beside the old man and got back in the Mustang. They backed out of the alley and drove back to Davenport's house. They came out without the briefcase, locked the garage door, got back into the Victoria and left. I never heard the Mustangs brakes squeak, I would have lost my hundred.

My first thought was to break into the house and find the briefcase, but better judgment prevailed. It was getting dark so I headed back to my new home.

I pulled up in front of the house cut the engine and got out. At the house next door a young man in a red plaid shirt and jeans, with a shaved head and arms full of tattoos, was sitting on the hood of his car drinking a beer. He waved and I waved back.

A young woman came out of the house with a beer in her hand. She had nothing on but panties and a bra. She was a little overweight with a small roll of fat edging over the top of her panties and her large breast spilled out of her bra. She wasn't a pretty woman, but she had those puffy red sensuous lips that made you forget about her lesser attributes.

She sat her beer down on the sidewalk, took his beer from him and sat it down beside hers, grabbed him by the hand and began pulling on him. He looked at me, shrugged his shoulders, jumped off the hood, grinned and let the woman drag him inside and close the door. The lights went off in the house.

Old memories crept into my thoughts. It had been a while.

I dozed off to sleep as soon as I hit the bed, but the nightmares jolted me awake less than an hour later.

I got up and switched on the TV. There was a movie playing I hadn't seen but I couldn't get interested. I thought of Mary and how much I missed those little late-night chats we had before making love, and that crooked smile she always gave me when she was amused at something I said. There was a part of me missing and I didn't know how to fix it. I longed for her companionship and warmth. She was my compass that gave my life direction and purpose. I felt like a ship without a rudder.

I remembered the good times I had with my son. When Cooper arrived he was a long-awaited joyful blessing. Now there was nothing but emptiness. I had eyed the .357 more than once with the thought of ending it all. Tonight was no exception. I finally managed to go to sleep a little before dawn for a couple of hours.

I had a light breakfast the next morning to make up for the fast food I ate the day before. I could see bottles of Jack

Daniels floating around in front of me. I was considering giving in to the urge when my phone rang. It was Goodnight.

"McKay, I checked out the tag number. The car belongs to a Simon Moore. He's one of the no-goods that deals to kids. We put him in the slammer about three months ago."

"If the Mustang doesn't belong to Davenport what's it doing in his garage?"

"The car is supposed to be in the police impound," Goodnight said.

"Well, it was in Davenport's garage yesterday. I don't know about now."

"I told Davenport to come in. He doesn't know why. I sent a patrol car out to Davenport's house to see if the Mustang was there."

"While you're at it, check out his partner. He and Davenport made a pick-up in the Mustang yesterday. There's a briefcase somewhere in the house; I think it's drugs. He left the house without it."

"I told you to stay away from Davenport."

"Sorry."

"What am I going to do with you, McKay?"

"Give me a medal."

"I don't think so, but I'll pick up Davenport and his partner."

"Let me know if you need me. I've got another call, talk to you later." I punched in the new call, it was Bobby. "You alright Bobby?"

"There is one little problem," he said.

My pulse rate began to rise. "What is it? You hurt?"

"No, it's nothing like that. Mrs. Morgan called me. Mr. Morgan died. The problem is she is going to move to an assisted-living apartment and can't keep the dog. Pepper's not a dog person and I need you to put him in a kennel for me temporarily."

"You scared the hell out of me, Bobby."

"I'm sorry, Colonel. I didn't mean to upset you."

"I'll do it as soon as I can."

"Mrs. Morgan is moving this week," he said.

"Alright. Don't worry about it."

"Thanks," he said. "Let me know how much it cost and I'll pay you back."

"Don't worry about it. You doing okay?"

"Everything's fine except for the dog," he said.

"I'll take care of it," I said. "Let me know if you need anything else."

"I'll do that. Bye, Colonel."

"Bye," I said and hung up.

27

Davenport denied everything. His excuse for having the Mustang was that he was using it to trick the drug dealers into thinking he was working with Simon Moore, or "Big Mo" as he was known on the street. Unfortunately, he didn't get authorization to use the Mustang. He wasn't supposed to be working drugs and he couldn't explain why he didn't turn the money in or make any arrest. There was also a repair receipt for the brakes in the Mustang glove box.

He wanted to cut a deal right away. He gave up his partner Mike Ridgeway as the man behind the drug deals and said he was only trying to get money to pay the loan sharks he had to borrow from when his wife was dying of cancer. Before any kind of deal could be made with Davenport, Overa got his deal and fingered Davenport as his accomplice in murdering the Spiciers. Davenport was up shit creek.

Overa said it was Coleman who gave them the contract on the Spiciers and showed them how to use the Trilene. Goodnight seemed to be shocked at what Davenport had done. I wasn't. His eyes were too close together.

That left Mike Ridgeway as the scapegoat for all the other charges. The D.A. wouldn't offer Ridgeway a deal.

Robert and Elle's murderers were under lock and key, but I still didn't have the file. Elton Parker kept popping up in my mind but I didn't have anything to go on but a gut feeling.

I asked Goodnight about the file again and he said the CIA said there wasn't a file missing. They had just misplaced it. There wasn't much he could do if the CIA said to drop it.

It would be a while before Overa went before a grand jury and spilled his guts about the crime bosses Goodnight wanted so bad. I wasn't sure what my next move should be, maybe it was time to pick up the dog. I wasn't a big pet person either but I could understand why the dog was important to Bobby since it had belonged to his dad.

I discovered there were over twenty boarding kennels in the phone book. I called one. It was almost as expensive to board a dog as it was a human. The size, weight and length of stay determined the cost. I didn't know how long the stay would be so I would have to put up a two hundred dollar deposit, plus the first month, in advance.

I drove out to the Morgan house. Maggie remembered me talking to her husband. I expressed my sympathy and thanked her for taking care of the dog. I offered to pay her but she said Bobby had already done that. She brought the dog to me. He didn't remember me and tried to bite.

I put him in the back seat against his protest and headed for the kennel. When I got there he didn't want to get out of the car. Fortunately Jack Russell Terriers are not that big. I was bigger and stronger. I grabbed him by the collar. He jerked his head away, twisted my hand in the collar and it broke. I left the collar in the car, forced him under my arm and took him inside.

The place looked like a doctor's office. It was very clean and odorless. It had white walls and expensive beige tiles on the floor. A young attractive receptionist was typing away on a computer with stacks of files on her desk. People in white coats and scrubs were coming and going through double swinging doors. A fortyish lady wearing a pearl necklace to accent her expensive designer dress was standing just inside the door holding a big German Sheppard on a leash. Scooter growled at them as we passed.

This was the high-rent district of doggie world. No wonder it cost so much. I walked up to the receptionist's desk, Scooter under my arm in a vise grip, and gave her my name. She rang a bell and a man in nursing scrubs came and carried Scooter away. He didn't like that man either.

"Fill out these forms for me, please," the young lady said.

I filled them out the best I could. I knew his name was Scooter. He was a Jack Russell Terrier, maybe ten years old, and a mean little cuss.

"Do you know when he was vaccinated?" she asked.

"No, he's a friend's dog."

"We have to have the date. He should have a tag on his collar."

"He does. His collar broke, it's in the car."

I went to the car and reached in the back floorboard for the collar. When I picked it up a key fell out of the busted end. The key looked like a locker key with the number 4273 on one side and the letters IBS on the other side.

I put the key in my pocket, took the collar to the young lady, paid the fees and left.

Sam was right. Robert hid the file. The trick was finding it. The endless possibilities were mindboggling.

28

I decided to have a hamburger at Landry's. I pulled up
to a parking meter about half a block from Landry's,
stuck the key under the edge of the dash for safe keeping and
got out.

I was putting money in the parking meter when two men
walked up. They were big enough to play tackle for the
redskins and ugly enough to scare the hell out of little
children.

One opened his coat and showed me a pistol stuck in his
belt. He tapped it with his fingers. His callused, oversized
knuckles told me he used more than a gun. He squeezed my
elbow till it hurt and shoved me toward a black limousine
with dark-tinted glass. "Come with us," he said. The other

one just looked at me with a nasty stare. They escorted me to the limo and relieved me of my .357.

"We'll keep this," the one tapping the gun said. "Get in, don't touch the boss."

The other one opened the door. I got in the back seat and my escorts followed. One got in the front and the other one slid in next to me.

A man I didn't know, maybe in his late sixties, was sitting on the other side of me. He had long, wavy black hair to his shoulders and a face as blank as a pancake. His dark brown eyes were hard and cold with no emotion in them. He gave me the feeling he could rip my heart out and never ask me my name. He had a small jagged scar above his right eye. He was wearing what looked to be an expensive black pinstriped suit over an overweight body. He had large hands tucked in smooth black leather gloves and a monogrammed white silk scarf draped around his neck with the letters M. D. on it. I was pretty sure it didn't stand for doctor.

He turned to me and the corners of his mouth turned up almost to a smile then quickly disappeared. He raised a gloved hand and motioned for the driver to go. "So you're McKay," he said in a raspy voice. "From what some of the boys tell me you're a pretty tough dude. You look fit, like you could take care of yourself. I like that. It makes it more fun when I see you go down."

Him thinking I was in shape was ironic since I was floating in Jack Daniels about half the time. "What do you want?" I asked, eyeing the door handle.

"I want the file that Spicier took from the Company. We don't want them to get it back or go to the FBI with it. You understand," he said, looking straight ahead as if I wasn't there.

"I don't have it."

"McKay, I made the mistake of sending people after you that were not up to the task. I underestimated you. Not anymore."

"Who are you?" I asked.

"Someone you don't want to piss off."

My phone rang. I reached for my pocket.

"Go ahead, answer it," he said. He watched while I raised the phone to my ear.

"Hello," I said.

"It's Bobby, Colonel. Don't listen to them."

"Are you alright, Bobby?"

"Don't listen to them. Forget about me, take care of yourself," he said.

"That's enough, McKay." He took the phone from me and closed it before pitching it back to me. "Don't try to trace the call. It was made from a pay phone. We took out a little insurance in case you wanted to be difficult. He's a dead man if you don't give us that file. We don't intend for the Company to get their hands on it again. They might not be as corporate as in the past."

"I don't have the file, but I may be able to find it. Just don't hurt Bobby."

"Alright, I'll give you a chance to save the boy. It's 5:30 now. Bring the file and meet us in the parking lot of Big Lou's Spaghetti House at 20 Third and Carver at 8 sharp tonight. You don't show up, he's dead."

"I don't know if I can find it that soon. I need more time."

"That's all the time you have," he said. "I'm tired of worrying with you." He waved his hand toward the curb and the driver slowed down, pulled over and stopped.

The guy sitting next to me got out and motioned for me to follow. He handed me the .357 with one hand, the bullets with the other and grinned. "I'm going to take this off your dead body next time." He got back in the limo, closed the door and they drove away.

I hailed a taxi and picked up the Super Sport. I stopped at Wal-Mart to buy some folders and a big envelope and made me a fake file – maybe it would work long enough for me to get Bobby.

29

I arrived at Big Lou's at exactly eight, parked and cut
my lights. I checked my weapon and waited. I may
have to shoot my way out.

My cell phone rang. "Hello," I said.

"You double-crossed me. We got word that you gave the
file to Terrell. He wouldn't give it to us. Here's what happens
to people that don't corporate."

"I didn't give it to him," I said. "Don't hurt Bobby."

He hung up. I heard a car engine start and squealing tires
from a black Cadillac roared around the corner into the
parking lot, headed straight for me. I jumped out of the car
and rolled behind a large tree. The Cadillac shivered, just
missing the Super Sport, me and the tree. The back door

swung open and a body came flying out and rolled across the black top. The Cadillac never slowed as it weaved its way out of the parking lot and was gone.

As I got closer I saw it was Rick Terrell, or what was left of him. His hands were tied behind his back. Three fingers were missing on his right hand. His right ear had been cut off and stuffed in his mouth. I got in the Super Sport and took off.

A block away, I glanced in my rearview mirror and saw the car that dumped Terrell gaining on me. I punched the Super Sport and pulled away from him. He kept coming. I heard the sound of breaking glass and then wind rushing through my rear window. There would be one hell of an explosion if they hit the gas tank. I was doing ninety and the Cadillac was gaining on me. I made a quick turn down an alley and came out on another street, made two more turns and the Cadillac was gone. They would be back.

I tried to call Bobby's phone but no answer. I doubled back to Big Lou's. There was no sign of the Cadillac. My next thought was answered when my phone rang a few minutes later.

It was Goodnight. "Colonel, I got bad news," he said. "I got a call from the LAPD. They answered a disturbance call and found Bobby Spicier shot to death at his apartment in LA. The police discovered his Washington connection and called me."

"Oh no. It's my fault. It's about that damn file. That son of a bitch was going to kill him anyway. I should have kept him here to protect him. He may have been murdered in LA," I said, "but the man behind it kidnapped me and Bobby. He let me talk to Bobby on the phone and gave me three hours to bring him the file before he murdered him. I don't have the file or know where it is. I don't know who he was but he had MD on a scarf and on his limo."

I thought better of telling him about Terrell. I'll let the police discover him.

"That would be Marcus DeAngelo," Goodnight said. "He's a mob boss. We know he's behind most of the crime in this town but we can't get anyone to talk. I'll see if I can get a warrant on him. Pass on my condolences and be ready to testify against DeAngelo."

"I will," I said and hung up. I didn't need a warrant.

I was down to two friends. A high-spirited young woman with a chip on her shoulder and a blue steel revolver that belonged to a dead man.

30

Picking up the phone was like lifting a three-hundred-pound weight. It took every bit of strength I had to make the call.

When she answered I blurted it out. "Pepper I got bad news, the mob killed Bobby. I tried to get him out but I failed. I'm so sorry."

There was silence on the phone for several seconds. "What happened?" she asked.

"The mob killed him when I couldn't give them the CIA file. They thought I was lying. I don't know where it is. I told them that and they killed him anyway."

"Why didn't you call me when they kidnapped him?"

"I thought I could get him out." I could hear her crying.

"I'm dumbfounded," she said. "You should have called me to help you. I didn't agree with his lifestyle but I loved him. He was my brother."

"Yes, I know. I loved him too."

"We should have let the pros handle this from the beginning, Colonel. We were wrong."

"Maybe so. What can I say?"

"Call Aunt Sara for me please. Tell her I'll call her later, I need to get myself together. I don't know what to do first."

"I'll call her, but you need to get out of the house. They may be coming after you. I told Goodnight to have Bobby's body shipped to the same funeral home Robert and Elle were in. I'll call you when he gets here."

"I'll go to Matt's place. Call me," she said.

"I will," I said. She was gone.

When Sara answered the phone I suddenly went mute. I couldn't get a word out. My tongue felt thick, my lips were sticking together. I couldn't open my mouth. She said hello four times before I could speak.

"Sara, it's Clark McKay. Pepper asked me to call. Something bad has happened to Bobby. He's been murdered in LA." I heard her phone hit the floor. I held the phone and waited. A voice came on the line I didn't recognize.

"Hello, who's this?" the voice asked.

"This is Clark McKay. Put Sara back on the phone."

"Here she is. She passed out. What did you say to her?"

"Sara...you there?"

"Yes, I'm here. That was one of my boarders. I conked out. The shock was too much."

"I'm sorry. Can you talk?"

"Yes. What happened?"

"Robert and Elle were in trouble with some very bad people. That's why they were killed. The killers thought Bobby had something they wanted. He didn't but they killed him anyway. I'm trying to find out why. I'll tell you about it when I know. I talked to Pepper; she asked me to call and said she would call you later. They're sending Bobby's body to the same funeral home Robert and Elle were in. I'll let you know when he arrives."

"Somebody is wiping out my whole family," she said.

"I know. As a precaution I think it would be good if you got out of town for a while. Some place unknown to anyone else. You have my number if you need me."

"I'll do that," she said.

"Good. Call me if you need me," I said and hung up.

I took a quick shower, dressed and flopped down in a chair thinking about the key. I couldn't help Bobby, but finding that key would tell me who started all this and who would pay for it when I did. What did I3S stand for? I was certain the file was in whatever the key fit, but where was it?

My phone rang. "Clark, that you?" It was Sara.

My heart was in my mouth. "What's wrong, Sara?"

"I'm okay. I was so upset I forgot."

"Forgot what?"

"Bobby left an envelope with me when he came to Robert and Elle's funeral. I was supposed to give it to you if anything happened to him. I think he had a premonition or something."

"What's in it?"

"I don't know. He said no one but you was to open it."

"You think it will make any difference who opens it now?"

"Maybe not, but I promised."

"Okay, if that's what you want to do. Can you send it by FedEx or UPS? I'll get it in the morning."

"Sure, I can do that."

I gave Sara the address and apologized again for what happened to Bobby. She hung up and I sat there looking at the key. It was hard to believe Robert was a blackmailer.

Funny how you think you know someone. Trust them with your life, and find out you don't know them at all.

31

I was headed for Big Lou's when a familiar car pulled up behind me. It was the old brown Cadillac. It looked like the last of the Sanfinis had recovered enough to get his ass kicked again.

We got caught at a traffic light. I picked up the baseball bat, jumped out and ran to his car and knocked the driver side glass out, grabbed the inside door handle and swung the door open and was staring down the barrel of a large revolver. He tightened his finger on the trigger I dropped the bat and stuck my thumb in the hammer drop and caught it on the way down and jerked the gun out of his hand. I slapped him across the face open-handed. He tried to get out of the car but I slammed the door on his arm as hard as I could.

He grabbed his arm and let out a painful scream. "You broke my arm again you fucking nut!"

"That's just the beginning. Who sent you after me?"

"I saw you driving down the street, butt fuck."

"Where's your gay friend?" I asked.

"He left town."

"Only smart one in the bunch."

"Fuck you," he said.

"What does it take for you to get the message, Sanfini? You're not a tough guy. Are you naturally stupid or do you have to work at it?"

People were blowing horns, yelling for us to move. A big trucker guy walked up to me shaking his fist. "Get that car out of here dick head," he said.

"In a minute," I said, holding Sanfini's revolver up where he could see it. He got a frightened expression on his face and ran back to his truck.

"Give me your car keys."

"No way man," he said, holding his arm. I noticed two of his fingers on his hand still looked like broken tree branches.

I raised the revolver to his stomach. "The keys," I said.

"Here motherfucker," he said, handing me the keys. "I'm going to have you arrested for assault."

"You're unbelievable, Sanfini. Get your ass down the street before I stick this gun up your ass and pull the trigger."

"I'll get you," he said, holding his arm. "I'm going to kill you next time." He broke into a trot down the street.

"There won't be a next time!" I yelled.

A string of cars were blowing their horns and the drivers giving me the finger. I saw a motorcycle cop weaving his way through traffic behind me. Sanfini was shuffling down the street, favoring his left leg and holding his arm. I wiped his gun off with my shirt tail, tossed it and his keys in the Caddy, got back in the Super Sport and hauled ass up an embankment past the traffic.

32

As I pulled into the parking lot of Big Lou's Spaghetti House I saw the black limo with the MD licenses plate parked at the curb. He was here. I checked my .357, stuck it back in my belt under my jacket and wa ked in. I stood behind some people in a crowd waiting for tables and looked around.

He was sitting at the back of the restaurant with his two bodyguards nearby, a waiter standing near the table with a bottle of wine at the ready. He rolled a mound of spaghetti onto his fork and stuffed it in his fat face, held his glass up for the waiter to refill it.

I sat down at the bar and watched him from between two other customers sitting on barstools near me. A young, thin-looking waiter wearing a white shirt and a black bowtie appeared.

"What will you have sir?" he asked.

I almost said Jack Daniels. "I don't know what I want. Give me a few minutes."

"Very well," he said and walked away.

DeAngelo pushed his chair back and stood up. He motioned for his bodyguards to stay put and turned toward the restrooms.

A short hallway separated the restrooms from the dining area. DeAngelo walked to the men's room and went in. I got up and moved down the bar behind the waiting crowd to the restroom hallway. I saw a small A-frame sign sitting nearby that read 'Closed for Cleaning.' I nudged it over in front of the door with my leg and went in. I saw highly-shined black shoes under one of the stalls. There was no one else in the restroom. It had to be DeAngelo.

I placed both hands on the top of the stall door and jerked it off the lock and it flew open. DeAngelo was sitting on the commode; his pants down around his ankles, his coat hanging on a hook.

He jumped up. "McKay!" he shouted in surprise, reaching for his coat.

"Your turn fat boy," I said and jerked the coat off the hook before he could get it. I threw it out of the stall and a gun fell out and bounced across the floor.

He tried to hit me. I ducked and grabbed him by his long black hair and pulled his head between the open door and the door frame. I rapidly slammed the door on his neck as hard and fast as I could until blood gushed out of his mouth and nose. I kept slamming the door on his neck until he began to make gurgling sounds and his eyes rolled back in his head. I turned him loose and he fell to the floor, his naked white ass sticking up.

"That's what I do to people that don't cooperate." I reached over and flushed the commode. "You stink," I said.

It was all over in less than five minutes. I took off my bloody jacket, rolled it up, tucked it under my arm and walked out of the restroom and out the back exit door. There was no one in the parking lot. I got in the Super Sport and drove away.

Somewhere, Bobby was smiling.

Part 4
What's In
The Box

33

I had just finished my second cup of coffee when there was a knock on the door. I eased over to the window and peeked out. A UPS man was standing with a package in his hand. I opened the door.

"What can I do for you?"

"Are you Clark McKay?"

"Yes," I said, watching his movements.

"I've got an overnight delivery for you. You have to sign for it."

"If it's an overnight why wasn't it here yesterday? I was told it was mailed two days ago."

"You weren't here to sign for it yesterday. You have to sign for it. I can't leave it till you do."

"Alright, where do I sign?"

"Right there," he said, pointing at a line on the paper.

I signed it. He handed me the package and went on his way.

It was the package from Sara. I tossed it on the table and sat down staring at it. Maybe I should burn it and forget it. It's probably more trouble and I've had enough of that.

I had second thoughts, took a deep breath and tore open the package. I opened the envelope and a bank deposit slip fell out of a folded, hand-written note that read:

COLONEL,
THERE'S FIVE MILLION DOLLARS IN A SWISS BANK ACCOUNT IN MY DAD'S NAME. I FOUND THE DEPOSIT SLIP TAPED TO THE BOTTOM OF ONE OF THE FOOTBALL TROPHIES I TOOK FROM THE HOUSE. I KNEW IT WAS BAD MONEY AND SOMETHING BAD COULD HAPPEN. IF YOU'RE READING THIS IT DID. I KNOW I SHOULD HAVE TOLD YOU AND PEPPER. I'M SORRY.
LOVE,
BOBBY
PS: I'M GAY. I NEVER HAD THE COURAGE TO TELL YOU.

I picked up the deposit slip. It was a wire from New York to Robert's bank account in Switzerland. The sender was anonymous. I noticed a series of numbers hand written on the back. It appeared to be the code Robert and I used for our own purposes.

It was a simple code, not one for big secrets, but good for concealing things from the casual eye.

The code used the ABCs. A was one, B was two and so on. In this case it spelled 'Elton Parker.' Things were beginning to come together. It was dated a month before Robert's death. Robert and I taught Elle the code and we used it as a joke at parties and places where we couldn't say what we wanted to say out loud. We passed our pleasantries and laughed at things we said in the code. It was simple fun.

This wasn't funny. My good friend was a blackmailer and a fraud, his son was a thief and it looked like his wife wasn't as innocent as I thought. I knew what the key fit now and who had a reason to murder him.

The more I found out the more I realized there was even more to learn.

34

Goodnight was writing something on a notepad when I walked in. He looked up and seemed glad to see me.

"You wanted to see me," I said.

"You could have called," he replied.

"I thought I would make sure you were on the job."

"You're looking at me," he said. "I'm very sorry about Bobby, Clark"

That was the first time he ever called me by my given name.

"What do you want to talk about?" I asked, hoping it wasn't DeAngelo.

"The U.S. Attorney's office called this morning," he said. "Overa is scheduled to appear tomorrow before the grand jury. Since you brought him in, I could get you in to hear what he has to say."

"I thought you wanted me to get out of town. Why the change of heart?"

"We would be nowhere on the Spiciers and Sanchez murders if you hadn't brought Overa in. He would have been long gone."

"I don't know about that, but there are some people with a lot of punch in this town scared to death over what's in that file. And one of them is Elton Parker. I know he's involved, I just don't know to what extent. I think it would be a good idea to find out more about him. He may be in cahoots with the mob to get the file, which would include Overa."

"I'll see what I can do," he said. "Right now my focus is on Overa. He says he has a list of top mob bosses from Chicago to Las Vegas that he's going to give up with evidence to put them away if the government will put him in the witness protection program."

"I would put him face down in a shallow grave," I said.

"Well it's personal with you," Goodnight said. "I know how you feel, but it would be good to bring down some of those cocky bastards."

That was the first cuss word I ever heard Goodnight say.

"Something else – we found Terrell in the parking lot of Big Lou's Spaghetti House yesterday, carved up like a Christmas turkey and Marcus DeAngelo this afternoon in the restroom of the same place, dead as a doornail from someone slamming a stall door on his neck until his jugular burst and he choked to death on his own blood. You wouldn't know anything about it would you?"

"Nope, but it makes me happy."

"I figured it would," he said. "Give me a call if you want to come to the hearing. It starts at 9. I'll get you in."

"I'll do that," I said and walked out.

I think Goodnight knew I did DeAngelo but he wasn't too anxious to prove it. I think it made him happy too.

In this town everything is attached to either politics or money, and nothing gets done without both. The Overa hearing was no exception.

35

At nine the next morning I called Goodnight and told him I was coming to the hearing. I decided I would enjoy watching Overa squirm.

"There's not going to be one. He's dead," he said. "We found him hanging from a light fixture with his shirt sleeve knotted around his neck. He was in isolation and it looks like a suicide, but I think one of our own was paid to kill him."

"Good luck. I'm sorry for your sake, but I'm glad he's dead," I said.

"I know," he said. "I'll talk to you later."

I hung up and made a telephone call to Switzerland. After waiting on the phone for someone that spoke English they said I would need power of attorney and have it approved by the banking commission in Switzerland before I could open the deposit box or withdraw anything.

It was two in the morning before I could get to sleep. I had another nightmare. Only this time Mary appeared in it in Vietnam, walking along a dirt road toward me with her arms outstretched saying, "Shoot me, Clark. It's okay, go ahead. Shoot honey. I'm ready."

I woke up, put on some coffee, thought about a drink of whiskey and waited for the sun to come up. I kept seeing Mary and Cooper's face every time I closed my eyes.

The next flight to Zurich didn't leave until three that afternoon. I called Pepper and told her about the note I got from Bobby and that I thought the file was in the deposit box.

"You may be right, Colonel," she said. "We need to go to Switzerland."

"I think it would be better if you stay with Matt. Make me out a power of attorney so I can get in the box and I'll go check it out. Call Goodnight if you have any trouble."

"Alright, I'll have it ready when you get here with death certificates for validation." She gave me Matt's address and hung up.

I picked up the power of attorney papers from Pepper and looked up the paint and body shop with the largest phone book ad, called and made an appointment to drop the car off. When I got there the body man looked it over and said it would take a week to ten days to fix it. He asked what the stains on the seats were. I told him I didn't know. The cost was ten thousand if I wanted it to look original. What the hell, it was only money. I told him it was a deal if he would take me to the airport. I gave him a check for a thousand dollar advance and he drove me to the airport.

I ate and bought a travel bag, pants and shirt. I stuffed the power of attorney papers, passport and deposit slip in my pockets and dozed for the next three hours. When it came time to board the flight I was wide awake. I hoped they had a movie.

When we landed in Zurich, I wasn't on the ground twenty minutes before I started noticing the lack of oxygen from the altitude. I caught a taxi to the hotel, checked in and called the bank. A man answered in German. I asked to speak to someone that could speak English. A woman came on the line, she said her name was Nina. She repeated the same thing I heard before. I would have to present my papers to the banking commission office at the capital in Bern before the bank could honor my power of Attorney.

It was too late today to get to Bern, so I exchanged some American dollars for Swiss francs at a too-high rate, had dinner and went to bed. I tossed and turned all night, thinking about Mary and Cooper. I thought about calling Mary's sister Billie while I was in Europe. She lived in Paris, where she and my wife grew up as the daughters of a U. S. State Department diplomat.

It was at one of those diplomatic parties that I met Mary while serving a tour in Germany. She had just returned from graduating college and flaunting her newly-acquired title of 'Miss Springdale' when we met. She planed to go into diplomatic service like her dad, but after we married she became a teacher for the rest of her life.

Billie was an accomplished artist and sold some of her paintings for over a hundred thousand each. She never got married. No one was sure why. She seemed to have lots of boyfriends but none she wanted to spend the rest of her life with.

Their father died from a heart attack in the Eighties and their mother in a nursing home after a paralyzing stroke. Billie blamed me for Mary and Cooper's death. Maybe I should let sleeping dogs lie, as they say.

I woke up the next morning feeling dizzy, with more altitude sickness. I knew it would take another day or two to become acclimated.

I caught a train to Bern and enjoyed the breathtaking scenery, until I noticed a man I had seen at the train station paying more-than-casual attention to me. He spoke to the conductor in German. He looked to be in his forties, with a dark complexion, glasses, and wearing a European-styled brown suit. I moved to another car and he followed.

When we arrived in Bern I had a taxi driver make the block and return to the train station. The man on the train followed in his taxi.

I went in the bank and headed for the restroom, pulled off my belt and waited by the door. When he walked in I looped the belt around his neck, yanked it tight, dragged him into a stall and pulled his gun out of his shoulder holster.

"Why are you following me," I said, tightening the belt.

He grabbed at the belt trying to pull it loose. I tightened it some more. His glasses fell off and his eyes bugged out like two fried eggs.

"Pocket," he said, gagging. "Badge in pocket," he said with a thick German accent.

I stuck my hand in his coat pocket and retrieved a badge that appeared to be a policeman's badge.

"You're a policeman?"

He shook his head yes, gasping for breath. I loosened the belt and shoved him out of the stall.

"What do you want with me?" I asked, holding his gun.

He bent over his hands on his waist. When he had regained his breath he straightened up. "We have information you are here to pick up drug money."

"Where did you hear that?"

"From an informant is all I can tell you," he said, rubbing his neck.

"If the money is drug money that's news to me," I said, handing him his gun and glasses.

"We cannot let you have the money until we check everything."

"Am I under arrest?"

"You assaulted a policeman but I will let that go considering the circumstances." He stuck the gun back in the holster and put his glasses on.

"I'm wasting my time with the banking commission, right?"

"I would say yes," he said. "Enjoy our beautiful country and when we have come to a conclusion, we will let you know."

"How long will that be?"

"A month, maybe two," he said. shrugging his shoulders.

"If Parker thinks this is going to stop me he's wrong."

"I do not know anyone named Parker. I was told to put you under surveillance by my superior."

"You can quit following me, I get the picture."

"Take a vacation. Go home and forget the money," he said. He straightened his coat and tie and walked out ahead of me, disappearing into the crowd.

Parker had trumped my hand but the game wasn't over. He could have the money, I wanted in the deposit box. That was where the file was and he knew it.

The more I learned about Parker the more I was convinced he was my man. He was the one behind it all, from the mob to the CIA. Proving it would be the hard part. If I could find the file Robert stole maybe I could nail him. That is, if I lived long enough. I was beginning to feel like a duck in one of those carnival target games where the duck goes back and forth and everyone tries to shoot him.

36

My ride back to Zurich was a little less nauseating. I was beginning to adjust to the altitude.

I stopped at the bank and asked where the deposit boxes were. The cashier said, in broken English, I would have to be cleared by a bank official before they could let me in the vault. I gave the cashier my name and asked to speak to Nina. The cashier picked up a phone dialed a number and spoke to someone in German.

"She come soon," she said and gave me a smile. A few minutes later a pretty young woman with short brown hair and blue eyes, wearing a conservative dark blue suit, white high heels and diamond ear rings dangling from her ears came toward me.

"I am Nina. I spoke with you yesterday, Mr. McKay. What can I do for you?"

"You speak very good English."

"Some people don't think so. I'm from New York," she said.

"I thought I detected a foreign accent," I said with a quick smile. "I need to get in a deposit box. The box is in my friend's name but he's deceased. I have the key, death certificates and power of attorney from his daughter, the sole surviving member of the family."

"Did you get authorization from the commission?"

"No. But I don't want to withdraw the money. I just need to see what's in the box."

"I am sorry, I can't do that. It would violate international banking codes and get me fired."

"Well what about if you go with me and let me look at the contents. I promise not to take anything out."

"I can't do that either, that's the same thing."

"Miss, I have reason to believe that what's in that box can help me solve a family's murder. I need to know what's in the box."

"Are you a policeman?"

"No, but someone ordered the murder of my best friend, his wife and son. I think the answer is in that box. Help me."

She looked at me, rolled her eyes and tightened her lips. "Are you telling the truth?"

"I swear it," I said, raising my right hand in a swearing stance.

"Put your hand down. Follow me. Just look, you can't take anything."

"Thank you," I said.

She led me past several desks to an open vault with rows and rows of deposit boxes.

"What's the name and number?"

"Robert and Elle Spicier, #4273."

We stopped in front of the box. I handed her the key. She opened it and handed the key back to me.

"You have two minutes," she said, folding her arms.

I pulled the box out and saw two jewelry boxes, a stack of thousand-dollar bills, and the picture he sent me of me, Robert and Sam in Nam. On the back was a notation that read, 'It's raining cats and dogs and no dog house.' That was the same thing on my picture. Nothing that looked like a file was in the box.

"Can I take the picture? It's a keepsake," I said.

"You can't take it. That was our deal."

"It's just a picture. It only has meaning to me."

She looked at the open drawer, then me. "You're making my job difficult, Mr. McKay." She studied me for a moment, sighed and shook her head. "I hope I'm a good judge of character. When I come back I want you gone, understand? The picture better be the only thing missing."

"I won't forget this."

"I hope I can," she said and walked away

I took the picture, put it in my coat, closed the box, stuck the key in my pocket and hurried out of the vault. Nina was standing with her back to me, talking to another woman when I left.

"Who said New Yorkers were cold. I may have to send her some flowers or something."

37

When I got to my hotel room I took the picture and laid it on the bed.

Why would he put that picture in a safe deposit box, I thought. Does our last day in Vietnam mean something I don't know about?

The only thing I remembered from that day was the pouring rain and Sam trying to get someone to take a picture with his camera of us holding a poncho over our heads for a souvenir. He finally did. He had it developed and gave me and Robert an 8x10 copy. It wasn't a very good picture but you could make us out.

I went to the bathroom and ran water over the picture, back and front, and all it did was shrivel up. Maybe the clue is in my picture?

The phone rang four times before Billie answered it.

"Billie, it's Clark. What did you do with the picture of me and my buddies standing under a wet poncho?"

"What're you talking about Clark? I haven't heard from you since we buried my sister and nephew and now you call me and start babbling about something I don't know anything about."

"It was in the things you took back with you. The keepsakes I asked you to keep for me. Pictures of Mary and Cooper and one with me and my buddies standing under a poncho, that's the one I need. I'm sorry to bother you Billie. It's important. Where is it?"

"I think it's in one of the boxes with some other things."

"Go check for me and call me back on my cell phone please."

"Why such a hurry?"

"I'll explain later."

Twenty minutes later my phone rang. "I found it, now what?" she asked.

"Take the back off very carefully and see if there's anything on the back of the picture or in the frame."

"Okay hang on just a minute." I held the phone and waited. "I'm back." She said. "There's nothing here but a notation on the back of the picture that says 'It's raining cats and dogs and no dog house.'"

"That's it, nothing else?"

"That's it," she said.

"I'm going to catch a train to Paris and pick up the picture. I'll see you this afternoon." "This afternoon? Where are you Clark?"

"I'm in Switzerland."

"What are you doing in Switzerland?"

214

"I'll tell you when I get there."

When I got off the train I flagged down a taxi and used what little French I knew to get to Billie's. I had forgotten the charm of Paris, with its cobblestone streets, streetside cafés, old unique houses and the smell of fresh bread baking.

I pressed the apartment number button on the gate and a green light came on. "Billie it's me, open up."

Seconds later, the gate came open, and I walked up to the vine-covered door of apartment 116 and waited. I heard the latch and Billie let me in.

"What are you doing in Switzerland?" she asked.

"It's a long story; where's the picture?"

"I'll get it." She went away and returned with the picture.

I took the picture out of the frame. I didn't see anything unusual about it either. I tried the water thing – nothing. If there was a message I wish he would have just told me. Who the hell did he think I was, Sherlock Holmes? Maybe the picture didn't mean anything and it was just something he thought a lot of. What the hell did he do with the file?

Parker would know what was in the file. To hell with this, it was time to go home.

"Billie, if anyone asks I was never here. That's the best way to keep you out of trouble. You understand? I was never here."

"You were never here. What's going on? Are you in trouble with the law?"

"No, it's nothing like that. I have to go. I'll explain when I have more time."

"Clark, I'm sorry I was so rough on you at the funeral. It wasn't your fault. I know that now."

"You were right. I should have never sent Mary to the airport. It's something I will never get over."

"You have to turn it loose sometime, Clark. You're welcome here. Come see me, I think it will help both of us." She gave my hand a gentle squeeze. She looked so much like

Mary with those same big, beautiful blue eyes that continuously haunted me.

"Thanks. I'll do that."

I hurried out and waved down a taxi. The taxi driver was wearing a black beret, and had a pencil-thin mustache and a pointed chin. He looked like a character from one of those French skunk cartoons.

"Take me to the airport," I said.

"Oui, Monsieur. Yes airport," he said. "I speak good English, no?"

"Yeah, great. Let's go."

I called Pepper on the way to the airport. "There was mostly money in the box, no file," I said. "There was a picture in the deposit box of me, your dad and Sam that raised my curiosity. I'm not sure why it would be there."

"Me either," she said. "I know in spite of the war that was one of his favorite times." "I'm going to New York to see Parker and find out what he knows about all this."

"If you need any help call me," she said.

"I will. I'll be in touch. Watch for the bad guys."

"I'll do that."

The next flight out was to New York City. I took it.

38

I picked up a rental at the airport and headed upstate. The drive was a little longer than I thought. The town was tucked away in a beautiful green valley with miles of dairy farms and the smell of manure everywhere.

The Long Shore city limits sign read 'Population: 25,054.' There was a look-alike square that you see in almost every small town, no matter where it is, with most of the downtown buildings empty.

Things changed as I left the downtown area. New businesses were being built, including a bank and a new elementary school with ELTON PARKER ELEMENTARY plastered across the front.

Like most small towns, the new part of town had moved away from the decaying old downtown.

An exception to the new construction was a restaurant named "The Coffee Cup." It looked like it had been around for a while. The building was old with a new coat of white paint, trimmed in bright red. 'COFFEE CUP CAFÉ' was painted in large red letters on the front. A sign in the window read 'HOME OF MA'S FAMOUS APPLE PIES. COME IN AND TRY A PIECE.'

There were only two customers in the place. A middle-aged bald-headed guy drinking coffee and eating the famous pie, and a young buck making goo-goo eyes at a pretty little waitress wiping down tables. Another waitress was sitting at the cash register watching the two young ones practice their mating ritual with a big smile. She was attractive with sparkling hazel eyes, long brown hair tied back with a red ribbon, and bright red fingernails, probably in her early forties.

"What will you have?" she asked, getting up from her chair.

"A cup of coffee, please." I sat down on a stool.

She poured a cup of coffee and sat it down in front of me. "There you go. Anything else?"

"Just some information. Would you know where I could find Elton Parker?"

"Who don't know the Parkers? They own everything around here except this café. And Ma won't sell."

"I see. And Parker – where is he?"

"Keep going north four miles down the road you're on, you'll run right into it. Big sign, has *PARKER DAIRY* on it, can't miss it."

"Seems like an unusual place for him to be."

"Don't know. I think he inherited it from his old man. Maybe sentimental about it."

"I wouldn't think Parker could be sentimental about anything."

"You a friend of his?"

"Never met the man."

"Didn't think so. You don't sound like you're from around here."

"I'm not."

"He used to come in and get a piece of Ma's pie every once and a while. Kind of stays to himself now, except when that boy of his comes to town."

"Why is that?" I asked.

"Boy's a state senator. They do a little politicking. People say Junior's going to be running for the big time next year."

"The big time? What's that?"

"The U. S. Congress. The House."

"Thanks. When I get back I'll have a piece of that pie. How much for the coffee?"

"On the house. You can pay when you come back for that pie."

"Thanks."

"It's really good," she said, licking her lips.

"I'll be back." I put a five on the counter and headed for the door. The young stud was watching the girl bend over the tables as she wiped them off, and she was making sure she gave him a good view. Hooray for young love.

At two-tenths over four miles, I rounded a corner and saw a huge two-story brick house sitting maybe fifty yards off the highway. It had big white columns across the front, a circle drive with no cars in it, two balconies – one on each end, Old Glory waving proudly in front of a white iron fence that stretched as far as I could see down the side of the highway in front of green hay pastures with a long white barn. Holstein cows grazed on the plush grass and there was a big sign the waitress told me about at the gate with Parker's name on it. Cameras were mounted on each side of the gate.

Two men in uniform stood inside the closed gate next to a little guard house. Both were packing. One had an old Peacemaker tied down like Wyatt Earp. I pulled up to the gate, shut the car off and got out.

"You got a visitor," I said.

"I see you," the one with the Peacemaker said. He was maybe six feet, well built, thirty-something with long black hair blowing in the wind. His green eyes seem to look right through me. He had all the traits of a Native American Indian except for a smaller nose. "What you want, fella?" he asked.

"Take me to your leader," I said.

"You trying to be funny?"

"Yep."

"You're not," he said.

The other guard walked up and stood looking at me, with his hands stuck in his belt. He was a little older with a beer belly, smaller. A .45 on his hip.

"What do you need to see the old man about?" The Indian asked.

That was what Sam said. Maybe they were one in the same. "That's between me and him," I said. "You can tell him it's about Robert Spicier."

"Is that supposed to mean something to me?"

"Not to you. It should mean a lot to him."

"I bet you're one of those civil liberty lawyers always coming around accusing the old man of not paying the farmers. Get the hell out of here before I kick your ass," the Indian said.

"Calm down, Brandon," the other man said, moving between him and the gate.

"I think you better go," the other guard said.

"Not until I see Parker," I said, staring at the Indian.

Suddenly a voice came out of the air. It was the intercom. "Who's at the gate, Brandon?"

He flipped a switch and spoke into the intercom. "Some asshole I was about to throw off the property."

"What does he want?"

"Tell him it's about Spicier," I said.

"He says it's about Spicier."

"Robert Spicier?"

I nodded yes.

"He says yes."

There was a short pause and a crackle from the intercom. "Let him in, Brandon. I'll take care of it. You stay at the gate and send Jesse with him to the house."

"Okay," he said. He unlocked the gate and barely opened it wide enough for me to get through. He placed his hand on the handle of the Peacemaker and walked back into the little guard house.

"We drive up or walk?" I said to Jesse.

"Walk. The boss don't allow any cars past the gate except the farm vehicles," Jesse said.

Why would you have a big circle drive if you didn't allow cars on it, I thought. Oh well, to each his on.

The door swung open as we stepped up on the porch. A thin elderly man with snow white hair, wearing a black suit and bow tie moved back and motioned us through the door. My eyes were immediately drawn to a large painting of Marilyn Monroe, then to a big man maybe in his late sixties or seventies standing on the marble-floored foyer. He had a full head of wavy gray hair and cat-like green eyes, like the guard at the gate. His shoulders drooped a little under the tan cashmere sweater accented by brown slacks and high-shinned soft brown loafers.

He came toward me showing a slight limp from his right leg and stopped a couple feet away. "Who are you?" he asked, staring at me.

"Clark McKay."

"Oh yeah, I've heard of you. Spicier was always making you out to be a hero. Most of the time the real heroes are left on the battlefield."

"I would agree with that," I said. "I understand you worked with Robert in the CIA?"

"Yes, in Panama. We ran across each other from time to time after that."

I was drawn back to the painting, it was so lifelike. "That's a good painting of Marilyn," I said. "She looks like she is going to step out of the frame."

"That's not Marilyn Monroe. That's my wife Beth. She died not long after that painting was finished."

"Sorry. She has such a striking resemblance to Marilyn Monroe, it's astonishing."

"That's what everyone says. Jess, you wait out here. I'll call you if I need you."

"Yes sir," Jesse said and leaned up against the doorframe.

"Come with me, Mr. McKay, we'll talk in the study." He opened the door and invited me in ahead of him, limped in behind me and closed the door. Thousands of books lined the walls of the huge, paneled room. A fire was burning in a large fireplace. He made his way to a magnificent hand-carved mahogany desk with a replica of an M-16 sitting on it, sat down and invited me to occupy a big black leather chair in front of the desk.

"I know this is not a social visit, McKay. What are you doing here?"

"I came to talk about money."

"Money. You want me to give you money?"

"No. I want to know why you gave Robert Spicier money. Five million dollars to be exact. That's what was in a Swiss bank account in Robert's name."

"What makes you think I would do that? I didn't know the man well enough to give him that kind of money."

"He put your name on the back of the deposit slip. That's not a coincidence."

"That doesn't prove anything," he said.

"I think he was blackmailing you with a CIA file that would send you to jail."

"You have this so-called file I should be afraid of?"

"No, I thought maybe you did."

"I don't know what you're talking about," he said.

"Murder, Mr. Parker. You didn't want to pay him anymore."

The thin man with the white hair appeared through a side door and stopped at Parker's side.

"Yes, Charles, what is it?" Parker asked, annoyed.

"Would you and the gentleman care for some refreshments, Sir?"

"The gentleman is not going to be here that long."

"Very well, sir," he said and marched away.

"A plump middle-aged Native American woman appeared through the same door carrying folded sheets on her arm. She gave me a curious look, walked to a door at the opposite end of the room, opened it and disappeared without a word.

"I don't know why I keep them around. They're not worth a shit. Wasted money," he said. "Now, where were we?"

"We were talking about the money you gave Robert and murder."

He leaned back in his chair and placed his hands on the desk, looking at me deep in thought. "You're implying more than you know, McKay. If you had any proof of anything you wouldn't be here. I've told you all I intend to. If you're trying to blackmail me forget it."

"I don't want your money, Parker. Just the truth."

"Go away and leave me alone," he said.

"If I find out you're responsible for his murder I'll be back and I'll be the judge, jury and executioner, just like Mike Hammer."

The veins in his neck popped out and his face turned red. He rose from his chair and limped around the desk. "Don't threaten me, you whiskey-soaked bum," he said. "Get out of my house this instant!"

"I thought you didn't know who I was?"

"I know all I want to know. Jess!" he yelled.

Jesse came flying through the study door. "Yes sir?"

"Escort this man off my property. If he comes around again, shoot him on sight."

"I'm going, but I'll be back," I said. "You don't have a very good poker face, Parker."

"Take my advice," he said. "Don't come back. You could have a serious accident."

"If I come back it will be for you."

"You think I got where I am by being stupid?"

"No, just greedy," I said.

"Get him out of here, Jess. Now! Before I shoot him myself!"

Jesse motioned for me to go out the door. "If you're smart you won't come back, Mister." "What happened to the old man's leg, Jesse?"

"Vietnam. He was wounded."

"The guy at the gate. Who is he?"

"Did you hear what I said, Mister?" Jesse asked. "You better listen. The old man means what he said."

"Yeah I heard you. Is that what everybody calls him?"

"Not to his face."

"Who's the guy at the gate?"

"Brandon. That's his mom, Lillie Two Trees at the house."

Brandon was watching us as we came down the drive. "You been running your mouth again, Jess?" Brandon asked.

"No! I haven't said nothing," Jess said, looking at me then Brandon.

Brandon unlocked the gate. "Don't come back, old man."

"You sound like an echo of your daddy," I said.

Brandon jerked his head toward Jesse.

"I didn't say anything, Brandon, I swear it," he said.

"Get out," Brandon said and shoved me through the gate.

"We'll meet again," I said. "Next time no more Mr. Nice Guy."

"Get on your way, blowhard," Brandon said.

"Why don't you go on, Mister," Jesse said.

"I'm going. I just wanted Chief Shit in the Face to know his day will come too."

I got in my car and hauled ass for town. I stopped at the Coffee Cup Café and had that piece of pie. It was so good I ordered a second piece to go. Sandy wasn't there. I liked her. I might have to come back for some more pie.

39

The next evening, I was returning home after buying Matt and Pepper dinner when I pulled up to my door and saw a shadow move swiftly across the window. It was no friend in the dark.

The only weapon I had was inside, and whoever was in there may have found it. I took off my belt, looped it through the belt buckle and wrapped it around my hand, inserted the key in the door, turned the lock and hit the ground.

Bright orange from a shotgun blast jumped through the open doorway, spotlighting the shooter for a brief moment. I charged before he could pump in another round and we went flying across the room.

I grabbed the shotgun, pushing the barrel up, and kicked him in the balls. He spun away trying to get the shotgun in position to fire. I grabbed the gun again by the barrel and stock, dropped to the floor, held on, kicked him in the gut and threw him over my head into the wall, losing my grip on the gun.

He fell to the floor still holding onto the gun. I gouged at his eyes, poking my fingers into both sockets. He yelled, cussed, and jumped to his feet. He staggered toward me trying to get his vision back, swinging the shotgun at me. I ducked, looped the belt around his neck, rolled on his back, dropped my weight on the belt and rode him piggyback across the room. He fell to his knees, made a gurgling sound, dropped the gun and fell to the floor.

When he didn't move anymore I let off the belt and turned on the lights. I didn't know him. I took a deep breath and checked his pulse. He wasn't breathing.

I called 911 and tied his hands just in case, then pushed the shotgun away and went to the bathroom and checked the empty commode tank to see if the .357 was still there. It was. I left it there, put the lid back on the tank and went to take another look at my attacker.

He had black curly hair, looked biracial, over six feet tall and underweight, with needle marks in both arms. I checked his wallet. A driver's license said his name was George Barberwitz.

He had thirty dollars, two credit cards with different names on them, a DC bail bondsman's card and a receipt from the Majestic Hotel in Washington.

I stuck the receipt in my pocket and put everything else back in the wallet and stuffed it in his pocket. He hadn't moved. He was dead alright.

The ambulance arrived and they loaded Barberwitz in about the time the police showed up. After the ambulance took off, the policemen handcuffed me and hauled me to the station and started throwing questions at me. I called Pepper and she showed up; they released me the next morning.

I found out during the questioning my assailant was a small-time crook with a long arrest record and a drug problem. The shotgun was stolen.

The police concluded, with Pepper's help, that it was a robbery and self-defense. I dodged a bullet again, literally.

I caught a taxi back to the apartment and hurried in to retrieve my .357 and some clothes. Thank goodness nobody had to pee. I stuck the gun in my belt under my jacket and locked the door. I slid a check for a thousand dollars, the door key, and a note that said I had to leave town under the landlord's kitchen door. I crawled back in the Super Sport and took off.

Time to find a new home.

40

I spent the rest of the day finding a new place to live and was unpacking when Baldona called. He said there had been a shooting and Goodnight was in the hospital, but was going to be alright. He thought I would want to know.

I got directions to the hospital and hurried off. The admittance clerk said he was on the fifth floor, room 531

When I walked in, I recognized his wife from the picture on his desk. I introduced myself. "I'm Clark McKay."

"I'm Julie," she said, extending a hand to shake. "I've heard a lot about you."

I took her hand and held it gently. "Unfortunately it's probably all true," I said.

"Hi," Goodnight said. "See what a mess I got myself in. I won't be giving you anymore advice." His left leg was in a cast, tied up to an overhead bar to keep it elevated.

"What happened?" I asked.

"I was too slow. Moving like an old man. Oops, sorry."

"No problem," I said and grinned.

"We were making an arrest," he said. "The guy grabbed one of the officer's guns and shot me before I could get out of the way. I took him down, but I got a bullet in the leg."

"You going to be alright?"

"I think so. The doctor said it looked like it would heal okay," he said.

"He's beating himself up for getting shot," Julie said. "Maybe you can talk to him."

"Hey, nobody's perfect. Well, maybe one. Just be thankful you're alive," I said.

"I should have been more alert," he said, shaking his head.

"I'll let you two visit," Julie said. "I'm going to get a cup of coffee." She smiled and left the room.

"Nice lady," I said. "You're a lucky man, even if you did get shot."

"I know," he said, looking at the doorway then turning his head back to me. "I have something for you." He picked up a large brown envelope from the night table. "I had Baldona bring this in. I figured you would be showing up." He opened up the envelope and took out a stack of papers and ran his finger over the top page.

"You may be on the right track with Parker. He got suspended for a month one time when he worked for the CIA, for beating up a guy that was making derogatory remarks about Marilyn Monroe. The man dropped the charges later when Parker settled with him, don't know for how much. He arrested two civil liberty lawyers and charged them with treason for suggesting communists had the right to their beliefs. He got a six month suspension for that. He was active in covert operations during the Cuban Missile Crisis, but all that's still top secret. He worked with your friend Robert during the Panama fiasco.

"He was drafted, wounded, and served two years in the army. He formed Armco when he got out and has made a fortune selling munitions to the U. S. and other governments around the world, some questionable, but no charges were ever filed. He was even an Ambassador at Large in the seventies. Your boy is quite a character.

"He fathered the son of his long time housekeeper, Lillie Two Trees. The son's name is Brandon Two Trees. Parker never officially recognized him as his son. The painting you saw may really be his wife. She was a dead-ringer for Marilyn. Don't know if she had plastic surgery. She died two years after Marilyn, from cancer. She was three years younger than Marilyn. I haven't found any connection to Overa yet. There's more in the envelope, nothing incriminating.'

He handed me the envelope. "I thought I would trade you," he said. "I need to ask a favor."

"Anything, just name it."

"I want you to keep an eye on Julie and the kids until I get out of here. I could put a uniform at the house but I think it would frighten them. The guy we took down has a brother that was making noises about hurting me and my family. Probably nothing, but I would feel better if I knew my family was being watched until I get out of here. If you run into any trouble call Baldona and he'll get a car out there, here's the address." He picked up a business card off the nightstand and handed it to me. "The address is on the back," he said. "I'll give Julie your number and tell her if she needs anything to call you. Just stop by every now and then to make sure they're okay."

"You got it. I'll take care of it."

"Don't hurt anyone. I'll alert the guys that patrol the area and give them your description. Most of the time people just talk and that's it."

"Don't worry about your family. No one's going to get near them."

"Thanks," he said. "I should be able to go home in a few days."

41

I was chomping at the bit to pay the Majestic Hotel a visit but I made a promise to Goodnight.

I checked the address on the back of Goodnight's card and drove out to a plush neighborhood ten miles from D.C. in Virginia. It was getting dark when I got there. The houses were too close together for my taste. They were nice but you could look out your window and into your neighbor's. I found the street and drove by. A minivan was in the driveway.

I called Julie. "This is Clark," I said. "I was just checking to see if you needed anything."

"I'm getting the boys ready for bed. You want to come by for coffee?"

"Maybe next time. Call me if you need me."

I tried to get some sleep, but the nightmares would have no part of it. I got up at two in the morning and drove back to Goodnight's house, both to have something to do and to give my demons a rest.

Everything looked peaceful enough. I made a U-turn, headed back down the street to go back to the motel when an old dark-colored Ford truck passed me going the other way. I watched in my rearview mirror as it slowed down, cut its lights, and stopped halfway between Goodnight's and the house next door. From what I could make out in the dark, a big man wearing sweats and a jacket got out of the truck and walked across the street toward Goodnight's house with something in his hand. I turned the corner, cut my lights and the engine, and coasted to the curb. I was hidden by the house on the corner.

I walked along the block, close to the houses, until I reached Goodnight's house. I looked around the corner and saw a man prying on a window with a crowbar. He saw me and broke into a run to his truck.

I caught him before he could open the door and slammed him into the side of the truck. "What are you doing?" I asked, placing the .357 against his head.

"You a cop?" he asked.

"There it is again. No, I'm the guy that's going to send you to hell. Turn around and put your hands on the truck."

"Kiss my ass, dude."

"Do what I told you." I grabbed his hair and slammed his head into the truck again. He draped himself over the hood of the tuck and I patted him down and took a .38 out of his waistband. "What were you going to do with this?" I asked, showing him the gun.

"Crack walnuts." He just looked at me and seemed bored.

I held my gun up where he could see it and dumped three bullets out of the cylinder, spun it and put the gun to his head. "You got a fifty-fifty-fifty chance I don't kill you," I said and pulled the trigger.

He peed his pants. "You crazy motherfucker!"

"I've heard that before too," I said. "You know whose house you were trying to break into?"

"Yeah, that bastard Goodnight. He killed my brother."

"What would you do?"

"From what I heard he had it coming."

I spun the cylinder again and placed it to his head.

"You sonofabitch!" He closed his eyes and gritted his teeth. "You wouldn't kill me for no reason, would you?"

"I have all the reasons I need. You're trying to hurt people I care for. I don't intend to ever let that happen again."

"What the hell you talkin' about, man? You're crazy!"

"Probably. I guess we'll have to wake up the neighborhood. Unless you're extremely lucky," I said, spinning the cylinder again.

"Wait," he said. "What do you want from me?"

"I don't have time for formalities, so I'll make this brief and to the point. If Goodnight or any member of his family so much as sneezes, you better be in another state. You understand?"

"Okay! Let me go, I won't come back."

"I don't believe you. I don't think you appreciate the seriousness of your dilemma. You have overestimated your ability to intimidate."

"Who the fuck are you?"

I spun the cylinder again. "Who knows what another spin will do. Is the cylinder loaded or empty?"

"No! Please man, I understand. I'm gone for good. I promise."

"Give me your driver's license so I know who you are. Goodnight has rules…I don't. You come back, you're dead. No questions asked, just dead. You got it?"

"I got it! I damn sure got it," he said, handing me his wallet. "Whatever you say mister."

I took his license from his wallet and held it up to read his name. "Alright, Mr. James Dugan, remember what I told you." I stuffed his wallet back in his jacket.

"Let me go, please," he said, eyeing the .357 in my hand.

A light came on in the house closest to us. I turned him loose. He flew around the hood of the truck and jumped in.

I tossed his .38 in the back of his truck and ran for my car. He was gone before I got to the corner. I quickly got in my car and drove away.

42

The Majestic Hotel was in the worst part of a partially-demolished street. An old neon sign hung over the three-story building with the letters E and L burned out of hotel. The old building was on its last legs. It would be fodder for the wrecking ball soon.

Two black hookers were working the corner by the hotel. The neon sign above them flashed 'HOT' as they waved at passing cars. A kid not yet in his teens was peddling cope to a junkie in the alley across the street. A wino with the bottle still in his hand was passed out in front of the hotel. The hotel doors were propped open with rocks. Trash was piled up in the vacant lot next door, and the rats were having a luau. I was glad I decided to take a taxi.

John L. Lansdale

An old black man with dark glasses, gray hair and a
straggly gray beard was sitting on a stool inside a wire cage.
The tap of my shoes on the dirty tile floor got his attention
and he looked up from a racing form as I approached the
cage. He pushed his glasses back on his forehead and put the
racing form down.

"What you doin' here man? You lost?" he asked.

"No," I said.

"You looking for a piece of ass or maybe some stuff?"

"I need some information."

"Sorry, fresh out," he said, picking up the racing form.

"I'll make it worth your while."

"Like how much worth?"

"Let's talk about it first. I need to know what you know
about a George Barberwitz."

"You a cop, dude?"

"No. People keep asking me that."

"Didn't think so. Some down south in your mouth. From
Alabama myself; or I was, forty years ago."

"What do you know about George Barberwitz?"

"The money," he said, rubbing his fingers together. I took
a fifty out of my wallet and held it in my hand. "You don't
want much information, do you?"

"It's got a twin if you tell me what I want to know."

"Sonofabitch skipped out on me, owing rent. Said he had
this big deal, was goin' to make a bunch of money. I figured
he's full of shit."

"Did he leave anything?"

"Stuff I took out of his room was junk. Ain't worth
nothin'."

"I'm afraid you're not going to get the rent."

"Lyin' motherfucker! What happened to the asshole?"

"He made one mistake too many."

"You got a name, mister?" he asked.

"That's not important," I said.

240

"Get that all the time around here," he said, grinning. "Well Mr. Not Important, I got a name. They call me Gizmo on account I fix things. Can't see to do it no mo' though."

"You said you had some stuff Barberwitz left. Can I see it?"

"Can't rightly remember where I put it, seems I have some memory loss."

I took another fifty out of my wallet and held it up in front of him. "Will this improve your memory?"

"I think it's coming back," he said, reaching for the fifty. He bent down, picked up a cardboard box and sat it in front of me. "Here it is, help yo' self," he said with a big grin.

I rummaged through the box. It was like Gizmo said, there wasn't much there. I thumbed through a notebook with bad poetry and scribbled on the back were the words *TWO TREE* and a phone number with a New York area code. I ripped the cover off and stuffed it in my pocket. "You can have the box back, Gizmo."

I called three taxis before I could get one to pick me up. The kid that was selling junk was staring at me through the open doors. Two young athletic-looking black men walked up beside him. The old man looked at them and frowned.

"Maybe you better wait inside, Mr. Not Important. The street ain't no place for a honkie...I mean a gentleman."

I heeded the old man's advice and waited inside until the taxi arrived.

The old man walked out of the cage, with the help of a cane, and hobbled to the front door. "Goodbye Mr. Not Important," he said as I climbed in the taxi. He held up the two fifties so I could see them and grinned like a chaser cat as the taxi pulled away.

43

Two Trees was a name too unusual to just show up in some junkie's notebook in another city without a reason. After trying the phone number three times and no one answering, I had the operator verify the number. It was a pay phone in a bar in Long Shore, New York called The Idle Hour. I didn't know they still had pay phones.

It was obvious Brandon sent Barberwitz. The question was did the old man know about it. The puzzle had some missing parts. What was the connection between Two Trees and Barberwitz? If Parker knew, why did he suddenly decide I should be done in by a junkie instead of his bunch? And last but not least, how much did Junior and Brandon know about what their old man was doing?

243

This was one I had to handle on my own. I had to make sure I kept Goodnight out of this one. I might have to do some things that would put him in a position of having to choose between me and the law, and I didn't want to do that. I would have to be patient and wait for Brandon to venture off the Parker farm before I could get him.

I decided to leave the Super Sport in DC, rented a car and drove to Long Shore, and asked questions about Brandon Two Trees. Where did he go? When did he come to town? What were his habits? Who were his friends? I didn't get many answers. No one wanted to be on Parker's or Brandon's bad side.

The older waitress at the Coffee Cup was the only one that would talk about the Parkers. She said Brandon usually came to town on the weekend to party at the Idle Hour bar down on 6th street. He got mean when he had too much to drink and scared the hell out of her one time when she and a girlfriend went to the bar. It was common knowledge that Brandon was Parker's son, but you didn't talk about it. Sandy said she heard Lilly Two Trees came off the reservation to work for Parker when she was a young girl and never went back.

I decided to see what the Idle Hour club looked like. It was dark inside. It took a few minutes to get my night vision. It was early evening, I was the only customer. I made my way to the bar and sat down. The place wasn't very big; ten or twelve tables, a bar, a small dance floor, a jukebox, and signs of different beer brands hanging everywhere on the walls.

The girl behind the bar was young, maybe too young, with big blue eyes and long blonde hair tied up in a ponytail. She had on too much makeup and a low-cut red dress that gave everyone a peepshow view all the way to her navel every time she bent over the bar. She looked like she should be at a high school football game, cheering for the home team instead of tending bar. I ordered a Coke and dropped a five on the bar.

A big burly man with long blonde hair, large biceps and a beer belly came in laughing to himself. He was already three sheets to the wind. He sat down two stools from me.

"Damn it's quiet in here. Let's get some noise in this place!" He staggered over to the jukebox and put in several quarters. I was surprised when country music started playing. For some reason I didn't think people in New York listened to country music. The Idle Hour may have been an exception.

He came back to the bar and plopped down hard on the stool. "Hey missy, bring me a pitcher of beer."

"I don't know, Gary, maybe you should wait a while before you drink anymore," she said, looking at the man sitting at the cash register. He nodded in agreement.

The blonde guy pounded his fist on the bar. "I'll decide when I've had enough, you little whore. Bring me some beer!"

The man at the cash register got up and walked out from behind the bar, holding a baseball bat with a looped leather strap tied to the small end and wrapped around his wrist. He was about as big as the blonde guy, with brown curly hair and a matching beer belly. He moved slow and deliberate toward the drunk and stopped about three feet away, leaning on the bat. "Get out," he said. "You're already drunk. Go home and sleep it off, Gary."

"Shit, Curley, can't a man have any fun anymore?"

"Go home. This is the second time I've had to chase your ass out of here this week. I'm getting tired of you and Brandon raising hell in my place."

The drunk got up, fumbling for money.

"You don't owe anything, Gary...now out." He used the bat as a pointer and motioned toward the door.

The drunk looked at the barmaid like he could strangle her and staggered out.

Curley sat the bat against the bar and walked over to me. "Sorry about that. This your first time at the Idle Hour?"

"Yep, first time."

"I thought so. Here, have a drink on the house. We don't want to give our new customers the wrong impression."

"Thanks but I'm good. This is all I wanted," I said, holding up the Coke.

"Gary can't hold his liquor," Curly said. "We got a lot of young bucks around here with the same problem. They think they have to prove what a big man they are by drinking everything in sight. I had the same trouble with him last weekend. He came in with Brandon Two Trees and a stranger. They proceeded to get drunk and harass my customers, making complete assholes out of themselves. Had to run them all off. I don't care if they ever come back."

"What did the stranger look like?"

"I don't remember much about him. Kind of tall and thin, with dark hair. Looked like he wasn't getting enough to eat. Why?"

"I just wondered." I got up, pitched another five on the bar and started walking out.

"Sorry about the commotion. Come back to see us."

"I will."

On the way to the motel a police cruiser pulled up behind me and turned on his flashers. Thank goodness I had left the .357 at the motel. I pulled over and stopped. They stopped behind me. A spotlight came on, blinding me. I heard the crackling sound of a microphone. "Get out of the car and stand next to it, keep your hands on top of the car."

I eased out and raised my hands over my head and laid my arms across the top of the car. One of the cops stayed in the patrol car while the other one moved up behind me and patted me down and told me to turn around.

"What you doing in Long Shore, mister?"

"Did I break a law?"

"I'll ask the questions," the cop said. "Let's see your driver's license." He looked at the license and frowned. "Texas, huh? You're a long way from home, Mr. McKay."

"That's a fact. Can I put my hands down?"

"Go ahead."

I put my arms down and leaned against the car and crossed my legs. That was the least-threatening pose I could take, I didn't want to give them an excuse to shoot me.

"You give us permission to search your car?" the cop asked.

"Do you have probable cause to search my car?"

"We'll decide that."

"Well you better be right because you don't have my permission, and if you do you're opening yourself up to a lawsuit."

"You a lawyer, spouting all that legal crap? We decide what's right or wrong around here. Get out of town. Go back to Texas, or wherever, just don't come back here."

"That's not very friendly."

"Don't mean it to be."

"You mean Elton Parker said I wasn't welcome here?"

"Old Man Parker doesn't have anything to do with it. You've been harassing people all over town, asking questions about Brandon Two Trees. That's an invasion of privacy in Long Shore. We have a quiet town here. We don't need strangers coming in causing trouble. If you're not gone by tomorrow we'll arrest you and give you a nice long visit in our county jail."

"On what charge?" I asked.

"We'll think of something." He handed me back my driver's license, walked back to his car and sped away.

When I pulled into the motel driveway I saw a big black limo sitting next to the office. A big man in a dark suit wearing a chauffeur's hat was standing at the back of the limo, smoking a cigarette.

I pulled into the parking space in front of my room. I sat in the car watching him in my rearview mirror. He smashed the cigarette out, got back in the limo and drove up behind me. He jumped out and opened the back door. A man got out. He had on a dark blue suit, a white shirt and red-white-and-blue stripped tie, with black wavy hair and those green cat eyes. He had to be a Parker. He must be the senator.

I climbed out of the car and watched him come towards me, the driver walking a couple steps behind him. "You Clark McKay?" he asked.

"Who wants to know?"

"Are you McKay?" he asked again, this time louder and harsher.

"Yeah, and you're Junior, right?"

"Yes, I'm Elton Parker, Junior. I want to talk to you."

"Join the fun. I just got harassed by two of your cops, why not you too."

"Can we go inside?" he asked.

"I'd feel better if you did your talking out here."

"Very well. I understand that you have some kind of thing against my father. I came to straighten it out. I'll make it very simple...how much?"

"How much for what?"

"How much to go away and leave my father alone. He's an old man and I don't want you bothering him anymore."

"You Parkers think any problem can be resolved by money. I don't want your money, Junior."

"Don't call me that," he said, tightening his lips.

"What *do* I call you? Senator?"

"Mr. Parker will suffice."

"Junior, I came here to find out if your father, or maybe you and your half-brother, had anything to do with

248

murdering my friends and trying to kill me. I don't intend to give up until I have the answer."

"I don't have time to stand in a motel parking lot debating with you, McKay. I admit my father is a bit eccentric, but he's harmless. I won't have you harassing him. Either you stop this now or I will stop it for you. Do you understand me?"

"Next time you come to see me, Junior, you better bring your posse because I'm going to stomp a mud hole in your ass. Do you understand me?"

The big man looked at the senator like a dog waiting for his master to say sic 'em.

"You're a violent man, McKay. But I can be just as violent if I need to be. You better take me serious."

"And you me, Senator."

He stared at me for a few seconds. "I can see talking does no good. We'll meet again, McKay, and it won't be pleasant for you. Let's go, William."

44

I paid a visit to the Coffee Cup the next morning and the waitress that was so friendly wasn't on duty. I remembered the name on her name tag was Sandy I asked one of the waitresses if Sandy came in later. She said she quit.

"Did she say why?"

"No," the waitress said. "She's been working here for six years, then called in and said she quit. Just like that No reason. We're going to miss her. Ma made out her check, she may be in later to pick it up." She poured me another cup of coffee and moved on to the next table.

I put a tip on the table and went to the register to pay. A check was stuck under the edge of the register with the name *Sandy Wiggins* on it. I paid my check then stopped at a convenience store and looked up Sandy Wiggins in the phone book. Her address was 164 North Elm Street. I asked the clerk for directions and found Elm Street.

A late-model red Honda Accord was sitting in the drive, with four flat tires and a broken driver-side window. A pink girl's bicycle was leaning against the porch with the front spokes smashed. There were no flowers in the yard and the house didn't have that well-kept look an owner gives a home. I pulled in the drive, got out, and knocked on the door.

Behind a closed door I heard, "Go away! I told you I would quit, and I did. Leave me alone!"

"It's Clark McKay, Sandy."

"Who?"

"The guy that was asking questions about the Parkers."

"Go away! I can't talk to you anymore."

"Open up, I just want to make sure you're okay."

"It's a little late for that."

I could barely hear her. I turned to walk away and the door opened.

"What do you want?" she asked, stepping out onto the porch. Her face was red, dried tears were stuck to her cheeks, and her hair was a mess.

"Who sliced your tires?"

"Who do you think? Brandon and his drunk friend Gary came by last night. Brandon told me to quit work and not talk to you anymore or they would hurt my little girl."

"Where's your husband?"

"Don't have one. You better leave before they come back. Brandon said he was coming after you. Better watch out, he's mean."

"Yeah, real mean, threatening women and children."

"Don't come around anymore please, I have to work. I got an eight-year-old daughter to take care of."

"Look, call the Coffee Cup and tell them you're coming back. I won't come around anymore."

"I don't know…I'll think about it."

"If you need anything I'm at the Sunlight Motel."

"Sorry, I'm just on edge. I know you mean well. Thanks for checking on me."

"If they bother you again let me know."

She nodded and closed the door. I took one last look at the Hondas tires for size and left.

I stopped at a tire shop and bought four new tires and sent the truck to her place to put them on.

I was sitting at a red light when Brandon's friend Gary made a left turn in front of me in an old Jeep. I followed him to a rundown apartment complex about two miles from town. A silver Ford Focus with a pizza sign on top followed me into the complex and stopped across the street. A little guy wearing glasses and a pizza hat got out and delivered a pizza. I swung around and pulled up behind him, cut the engine and got out. The pizza guy saw me and backed away. His knees were shaking. He was holding his hands halfway up like he wasn't sure if it was a robbery or not.

"Don't hurt me," he said. "I don't have much money but you can have it."

"I'm not going to hurt you. I want to buy a pizza…and your hat."

"I don't have any extra."

"I'll give you a hundred bucks."

"Boy, you must want a pizza bad. What kind?"

"Doesn't matter."

He reached in the open window of his car and pulled out two pizzas. "Here's two combos."

"Now the hat."

He handed me the hat and I handed him the hundred. He looked at me like I was crazy, mumbled something about quitting and hurried around to the driver's side, got in and took off.

I put on the hat and carried the pizzas across the street. Took the .357 out of my belt, held it against my leg with my left hand, and sat the pizzas on my open right hand. I couldn't get a good grip with my right hand because of my missing little finger. Guess fate has a way of adjusting things that need adjusting.

I rang the bell several times but he didn't come to the door. I held the button in and it kept ringing.

"Go away," he said through the door. "Quit ringing that damn bell."

"Pizzas," I said and banged on the closed door. The door came flying open.

"I didn't order any fucking pizzas," he said.

"Got an order for two pizzas and I'm not leaving until I get my money."

"Look hammerhead, I didn't order any pizzas. I'm going to kick the shit out of you if you don't go away!" He was in his underwear, his hair falling down in his face. Suddenly his expression changed. "Do I know you? Weren't you at the Idle Hour?"

"Yes, but we haven't been formally introduced." I dropped the pizzas at his feet and hit him on the side of the head with the butt of the .357 as hard as I could.

His head jerked back. Blood ran down the side of his head. He staggered back into the apartment, his knees buckling as he fell to the floor. I kicked the door shut with my foot, dragged him to a chair and tied him to it with a bed sheet. I threw a wet towel on his face. He moaned and shook his head, squinting at me with one eye. A knot about the size of a golf ball popped out on his head.

"Wake up Gary, we're going to play a little game. I ask questions, you give answers. Ready?"

He batted his eyes and shook his head. "What the hell did you hit me for? I didn't lay a hand on ya!"

"Would you have let me tie you to the chair?"

"Hell no."

"That's why I hit you," I said, placing the barrel of the gun to his forehead. "What do you know about a man named George Barberwitz?"

"Never heard of him."

"Wrong answer." I slammed the heel of my shoe on his bare foot. He let out a yell. "Be quiet, you're disturbing the neighbors."

"You broke my toe!"

"You have more."

"I told you, I don't know any George Bar... Barba... whatever the name was."

"If you don't tell me what I want to know I'm going to smash every toe you got, one by one."

He batted his eyes again several times and looked at me. "You were in the Idle Hour. You're that McKay fellow, aren't you?"

"That's me."

"I can't tell you anything," he said, squirming in the chair. "I got to pee."

"Guess you'll have to piss yourself." I stomped a toe on the other foot. I heard the bones break and he pissed on himself.

"You're crazy, you sonofabitch!" he said, gritting his teeth.

"I've been hearing that a lot."

"Man, I can't tell you anything. Go ahead and blow my brains out."

"Suit yourself." I cocked the .357 and stuck the barrel between his eyes.

"No, wait. If I tell you, will you give me time to get out of town?"

"Maybe. Depending on what you have to say."

"Shit, man, you're putting me in a hell of a bind."

"I'll put you six feet under if you don't start talking."

He shook his head and frowned. "Alright, point that damn gun somewhere else. Brandon said he needed a hitman, someone that couldn't be traced back to him. He gave me five thousand and said I could keep what was left over after I paid someone to kill you. I met this guy at a hotel where I went with a whore. I gave him two thousand and set up a meeting with Brandon at the Idle Hour."

"That was generous. Someone else does the dirty work and you make three thousand."

"I didn't have anything else to do with it."

"Well that was big of you. Do you know you can get life for conspiracy to commit murder? Did he say why he wanted me dead?"

"He said it was for his dad. You knew too much, you were dangerous. He wanted to do something to impress his old man. His dad didn't know about it."

"Tell you what, shithead, I'm feeling generous today. You figure out how to get out of that bed sheet and have your ass a hundred miles down the road in the next two hours and I won't turn you over to the police."

"I'm gone," he said.

"You better be." I stuck the gun in my belt and headed for the door.

45

It started raining when I pulled into the motel, and got harder and harder. It reminded me of Vietnam and the picture.

I called Pepper. "I haven't made any progress in finding the file," I said. "I've still got that picture on my mind. It can't just be a sentimental thing. He could have seen it a lot more at home. Did he ever say anything in reference to it, or about the circumstances of it?"

"Nothing I can think of," Pepper said. "But he would do some strange things every now and then. like building Scooter a doghouse. The dog slept with them and stayed in the house all the time except to go pee. When I asked him why, he said because all the other dogs in the neighborhood had a doghouse. Go figure."

"Did you say he built it?"

"Yes. He wasn't a handyman. That was out of character for him. He paid to have his lawn mowed."

"When did he build it?" I asked

"About a month before he was murdered."

"That's it. He put the file in the doghouse. That's why the picture was in the box with the notation and why he sent me a copy. Is the doghouse still there?"

"I don't know," she said. "I sold the house."

"I'll check and call you when I find out. Talk to you later."

Brandon would have to wait. I had to get to Washington as soon as possible.

I tore the picture up into little pieces and flushed it down the commode. I didn't check out so Parker would think I was still in town.

I caught a red-eye flight to D.C. and took a taxi to Robert's house and had the driver wait. I rang the doorbell and a young woman with a makeup mirror in her hand and hair up in curlers answered the door.

"Can I help you?" she asked, rolling her chewing gum around in her mouth.

"Yes ma'am. I was a good friend of the people who lived here before, they're deceased. They gave me their dog and I wanted to pick up his doghouse."

"Let me get my husband, I got to get ready for work. Buck, come to the door!" she yelled and walked away.

A little man with droopy eyes and shaggy hair, wearing a dirty white t-shirt, jeans, and no shoes came to the doorway holding a bottle of beer, stopped and tilted his head like he had one good ear, looked at me and waited for me to speak.

"I was telling your wife the people that----"

"Yeah I heard. I don't know about that. The doghouse was on the property when we bought the house. I think it would belong to us."

"Do you have a dog?"

"No, but we might get one."

"Tell you what, I'll buy it back. How much?"

He looked me up and down and took a swig of beer. "Five hundred should cover it."

"I would think so, about five times over."

"Take it or leave it, that's my price."

My first thought was to break his neck. "You know that's highway robbery."

"Not if you want it bad enough." A grin crawled across his face and he rubbed the cold beer bottle on his chin. I could kill him or pay him.

"Here's a check for five hundred," I said, taking my checkbook out of my coat pocket.

"How do I know the check's good?"

"Call the bank if you like."

He looked at the check, flipped it over, and then checked it again. "Naw, I trust you. I'll take it." He folded the check and stuck it in his jeans pocket.

"You got a hammer?" I asked.

"Yeah, I think so."

"Could I borrow it? Or do you want to be paid for that too?"

"No, you can borrow it. It's in the garage. What do you want a hammer for? The doghouse is okay...you're not going to hit me are you??"

"It's tempting, but no. You'll see." I followed him to the garage and he gave me the hammer.

The doghouse was sitting in the backyard, grass grown up around it. I took the hammer and began beating the doghouse apart.

"What're you doing!?!"

"Getting my money's worth." I knocked off the roof, pulled it apart, and there it was, wrapped in a plastic bag. I took it out of the crumbled roof, shook the dirt off, and handed the jerk his hammer. "I decided I don't want the doghouse. You can keep it."

"What am I supposed to do with that," he said, gesturing toward the pile of wood.

"You could stick it up your ass," I said, matter-of-factly.

"What was that you got out of the doghouse? Is that money? That should be mine you know. You just bought the doghouse."

I left him standing in the backyard looking at the demolished doghouse with a puzzled look on his face. "I'm going to cash the check," he said as I walked away.

By the time I got through with "Super Jerk" it was almost noon.

On my way back to town I made a call to the paint and body shop. The Super Sport was ready.

Part 5
The Last Stand

46

I saw it sitting out front when the taxi pulled in. It looked brand new. I was as excited as a kid with a new toy. The inside looked just as good. The owner of the shop came out smiling, wiping his hands on a rag. "Turned out pretty good. I can get you twenty for it today."

"I don't think so." I paid him the rest of his money and climbed in. It even had that new car smell.

I hurried back to my room and sat down with the file. It was a combination of several files, with parts pulled out and consolidated into a master file. The documents in the files had facts, dates, places and names, from the fifties through the Vietnam years, with Parker's name appearing over and over.

There were memos questioning Armco's shipments of arms to Panama and Vietnam. Bills of laden showing one amount being sent, and the receipts of the shipments showing a lot less, and nothing was done about it. Someone else was getting the missing weapons, and it may have been another country the CIA was propping up and hiding the shipments. Parker was right in the middle of it all. A thought I didn't want to face was that the missing arms may have went to North Vietnam through another country.

For some unknown reason, from the dates and subject matter it looked like they kept every scrap of paper like it was money, and Robert used it to create the smoking gun the file was now. The smart thing would have been to destroy the files.

A lot of the information in the files showed clear-cut illegal activities by a lot of people, and nothing was done about it.

A memo from President Kennedy to the Chiefs of Staff dated October of 1963 scheduled a meeting to discuss the withdrawal of a thousand troops from Vietnam by the end of 1963, and the complete withdrawal of all American troops at some future date to let the Vietnamese decide their own fate in a civil war that we had no business being in. That meeting never took place.

There were memos in the file showing the critics of pulling out of Vietnam rationalized that if South Vietnam fell to the communist all of Asia would, including Japan. It didn't happen that way and we lost over fifty thousand men and women in a war the military was not allowed to win for political reasons.

I stopped by Kinko's FedEx, made a copy, and mailed it to the director of the FBI with the president's memo on top, then went back to my room and called Pepper.

"Hello," she said.

"I got the file, it was in the roof of the dog house. I know now what Parker was afraid of."

"What do you think we should do with it?"

"I mailed a copy to the FBI but I'm not sure what will come of it. One way or another, Parker is going to pay for his part. I'm going to Long Shore in the morning, I'll tell you more when I get back."

"You want me to go with you?"

"No, I want you to stay clear of this. I'll call you."

"Let me know if you need me."

"I will, I'm going to try and get some sleep. Talk to you later," I said and hung up.

The damn nightmares came again. This time I saw the faces of everyone I remembered from the war. They kept jumping up in front of me like pop-up shooting targets. Next thing I knew, the faces were gone and I was walking alone down a narrow dusty trail between rice paddies, bodies scattered along the sides of the rice fields like discarded trash; the smell of decaying flesh whipping at my nose with every step.

Suddenly, everything disappeared like someone pulling down a shade. My mind had taken all it could take. I heard a noise. I realized someone was in the room.

I rolled off the bed and saw a man's shadow run toward the door. I jumped at him and missed. The shadow swung the door open and ran through. I chased him into the parking lot. I saw his arm point toward me. I hit the ground as a bullet whizzed over my head. A late model dark-colored sedan squealed around the corner and slowed down. The shadow opened the door with the car moving, got in and they sped away. The lights in the parking lot were too dim to make out the features or get a tag number, but I knew who it was. Parker had sent his henchman to get the file and kill me. Somehow I had survived.

Me and the Super Sport would take off for Long Shore in the morning and settle the score with Parker once and for all.

47

When I got to Long Shore the next day I decided I would visit Sandy first.

"What are you doing here," she said. "They're looking all over town for you. The police have been here twice. You're going to get me killed."

"You were the only one I could trust."

"What makes you think you can trust me? They passed the word around, anyone that tells the cops or the Parkers where you are will get a thousand bucks. Who would take care of my little girl if something happened to me? I don't have any family. I don't even know where that deadbeat ex-husband of mine is."

"You're not like them. You have courage to stand up to them. You're just out numbered. I'm going to even the odds a little."

"How do you know what I am? I've talked to you maybe three or four times. You don't know me."

"I know all I need to know, and I know you have to get out of here."

"I told you I don't want you around."

"Look, if you stay here they may hurt you and your little girl."

"I've got no place to go." A tear rolled down her cheek.

"I know just the place," I said. "Where's your daughter?"

"She's at school."

"We'll stop by the school and pick her up," I said.

"You're a walking time bomb, McKay. You know that? There's too many of them. It's just a matter of time until they kill you. What did you do to piss them off so much?"

"You don't want to know, but it's not over. Get your things and let's get out of here."

She looked at me for a second, closed her eyes and took a deep breath, walked to the bedroom, grabbed a bag, threw some clothes in it and then we took off for the school.

I made the block while Sandy went in to pick up her daughter. I saw her coming out and pulled over to the curb.

"This is Mary Ann, Mr. McKay," Sandy said.

"Hi Mary Ann. You're a very pretty little girl."

"Thank you," she said.

"We're going on a little vacation, Mary. You won't have to go to school for a few days. You'll like that, huh?" she said, smiling at the little girl.

I called Pepper.

She picked up the phone. "You alright Colonel?"

"Yes. I need you to do something for me."

"What is it?"

"A friend of mine and her daughter need a place to stay for a couple of days. I want you to pick them up at the airport and take them to Goodnight's house. I've already talked to them. I'll give Sandy Goodnight's address."

"Sure, when?"

"Today. I booked a flight for a 215 ETA in DC. Her name is Sandy Wiggins and her daughter Mary Ann. I'm going to pay Parker a visit as soon as it's dark at his farm."

"You want me to meet you there?" she asked.

"No, just take care of this and I'll take care of Parker."

"What do they have to do with Parker?"

"Nothing. They just got caught in the middle of this."

"Okay, I'll handle it," she said. "Don't you need any help?"

"I got it covered," I said.

"Be careful," she said and hung up.

"Sandy, a friend of mine will pick you up at the airport. Her name is Amanda Spicier, she will take you to another friend of mine, a policeman and his family. You will be safe there."

I took Sandy and Mary Ann to the airport and waited for them to board the flight. I felt better knowing Sandy and Mary Ann were safe and I could pursue the Parkers without worrying about them.

When they called to board the flight Sandy hugged my neck and Mary Ann did too. I was very touched.

"Don't let anything happen to you," Sandy said.

"No way," I said. "I have to finish the job. There's no one else. The ghosts of a lot of my comrades, and my best friend, are waiting for their revenge. I'll see you in DC."

48

I had just hit the main drag at dark thirty when Brandon came roaring by in his red Corvette, Jesse riding shotgun. I punished the horses and the Super Sport took off like silver. Two miles down the road I was right on his ass.

I caught up and clipped his rear bumper, throwing him into a spin. He left the road and wound up in a deep ditch. He gunned the engine, digging the tires deeper into the sand, going nowhere. I spun the Super Sport around to a quick stop with the lights shining on him. I jumped out and opened fire on the tires. The Corvette sunk further into the tire holes. I pointed the gun at the Corvette window, cocked the hammer, and motioned for them to get out.

"Get out now before I decide to pull this trigger," I said.

The engine stopped. Brandon pitched his Peacemaker on the ground and crawled out. Jesse tossed his gun out and followed Brandon's lead.

"Jesse you can go, my beef's with the Parkers."

"Thanks Mr. McKay. I was just doing my job, I don't want no more trouble."

"Go ahead, you coward, run! I don't need you," Brandon said and shoved Jesse away.

Jesse looked at me still holding his hands up. "Go," I said. He nodded, dropped his hands, and broke into a trot toward town.

"Won't do you any good to kill me," Brandon said. "The old man could care less. I'd be just another dead Indian far as he's concerned. I'm the bastard son. The old man will get you though. He always gets what he wants."

"Not this time. Did you know your good friend Gary Reed spilled his guts?"

"I don't think Gary will be talking to anyone else anytime soon," he said. "The police found him dead in his apartment this morning. The poor bastard hung himself."

"He probably had a little help tying the knot." Brandon shrugged his shoulders and glared at me. "Silencing the only one who knew you hired a hit man to kill me worked out well for you," I said.

"Well you know how hard it is to find good help these days," he grinned. "But in your case, you put that gun down and I'll show you I don't need any help kicking your ass."

"Beating up women and children makes you a coward, not a badass."

"Try me then. If you got the guts."

The longer I looked at him the more I realized how bad he needed a good-old-fashioned Honky-Tonk ball-busting ass-kicking. I could kill him later.

"Alright let's see how tough you are. Give me the keys to the Corvette." He reached inside the Corvette. "Easy now," I said, tightening my finger on the trigger. "Make sure the keys are the only thing you come out with."

He gave me a smirk and tossed me the keys. I motioned for him to move away from the car. I put all the weapons in the Super Sport, including mine, locked it and put the keys in my pocket, and patted the pocket. "Okay bad ass, come and get them."

"You just played hell old man."

He had a big grin on his face as he slowly moved toward me. Suddenly he reached down, grabbed a handful of sand and threw it in my face. He rushed in and clobbered me with a right cross, then a left as I staggered backwards, a little fuzzy. I ducked his next punch and kicked him away with a side kick. He fell against the Chevy, bounced off and charged again. I stepped aside, popped him behind the ear. He lost his equilibrium, staggered two or three feet, and fell down. He wobbled up to his feet shaking his head. I hit him with a quick right to the nose: blood flew across his face. Popped a hard shot with the heel of my hand between his eyes and he backed away rubbing his eyes.

"I can't see, you son of a bitch! What did you do?"

"You'll get over it."

He came at the sound of my voice, swinging wildly. I planted a strong right cross to his jaw and a hard kick to his balls. He shook like a wet dog and went down like a rock.

He was done.

I grabbed him by his collar, propped him up against the SS and gave him one last crushing blow to the gut. He threw up. I jumped back and let him slide down the fender of the Super Sport to the ground. He didn't move.

"Some badass," I said and pushed him facedown away from the fender. I got back in the SS, fired it up, turned it around and headed for Parker's farm. One down and whoever to go.

49

The gates were wide open. Parker knew I was coming. I wondered what kind of reception he had planned for me. I gunned the Super Sport and went speeding through the gateway. I pulled up to the front door, made a quick stop, jumped out with my .357 in my hand and Brandon's Peacemaker in my belt. To my surprise the door was unlocked and no alarm went off when I opened the door. He had something special planned for me.

The first thing that caught my eye was the painting of Marilyn, or whoever it was. I stepped lightly across the floor, moving further into the room. It was quiet as an Atheist prayer meeting.

A voice behind me broke the silence. "Don't even twitch, Clark. Drop your gun."

"Sam...you keep sneaking up on me."

"Drop the gun, Clark, last time."

I dropped the weapon and turned around.

"Stand real still," Sam said. He lifted the Peacemaker from my belt, kicked the .357 across the floor, stuck the Peacemaker in his belt and rapped on a door next to him.

"That you Sam?" a voice asked from behind the door.

"Yeah, we got a visitor."

I heard the lock turn.

"If you want to live a little longer, Clark, I wouldn't say anything bad about what you're going to see," Sam said. "And if it's any consolation, Robert was going to take the file to the FBI. His conscience got to bothering him, that's what got him killed."

"You're the one that told them about Robert being left-handed," I said. "You forgot he didn't shoot with his left hand. I saw the surprise on your face but I dismissed the thought, you being a trusted friend."

"You're wasting your breath, Clark, my conscience don't bother me," Sam said. A door came open and Parker stepped through into the study.

"We been expecting you McKay," Parker said. "Sam thought we might need some reinforcements, but I told him two well-trained men should be able to handle one hothead. I even gave the servants the night off. This is between me and you. I thought it would be our little secret, one you will keep forever."

"Suits me. I came to get the file or kill you, whichever comes first," I said.

"That's not a good start. He had this on him," Sam said, handing Parker the Peacemaker.

"How did you get my boy's gun?" Parker asked.

"I beat the hell out of him."

"Not in a fair fight. Where is he?"

"Lying in a ditch down the road. He'll recover."

"You won't." Parker put the Peacemaker in a desk drawer. "You should have taken the five million and forgot about the file. Sam said you would be here today after we took the file from you and here you are, right on schedule. You got more guts than brains, McKay."

"Money doesn't get the job done sometimes," I said.

"It always has for me. This time I'll see to you myself. That fool Coleman botched everything up sending those Sanfini morons after you and hiring that idiot Davenport to kill Spicier."

"I got the same impression," I said.

"Before we conclude our business McKay, or should I say before Sam ends it for me, I've got something to show you. You thought that painting was Marilyn, it is really my wife, but I'm a great admirer of Miss Monroe. Come in," he said, returning to the room he came out of.

Sam nudged me with his gun toward the room; I walked in. It looked like a museum.

All kinds of women's clothes were displayed around the room. A bright red dress hung on a mannequin in the corner, a poster of the famous skirt blowing up of Marilyn Monroe was on the wall, newspaper clippings, hair brushes, handkerchiefs, lipsticks, underwear, and pictures of Marilyn in all kinds of poses covered the walls.

A big bowl of ashes was sitting on a table next to an autographed 8x10 photo of Marilyn and Clark Gable from the movie *Misfits*. I knew the ashes were what were left of the file.

"What do you think," he said, sitting down in a gold colored lounge chair, excitement in his eyes. He was like a little boy on Christmas morning.

"Everything you see in here once belonged to Marilyn Monroe, even this chair I'm sitting in."

"Sam, you know this guy is nuts," I said, looking at Sam.

"For the kind of money he's paying me I don't care if he thinks he's Mickey Mouse."

Parker didn't even hear us. He was caught up in his Marilyn room. He was in another world. "I met her in New York," he was saying. "Such a charming woman. It was love at first sight. She invited me to come to Hollywood. I didn't get to go before she died. I always regretted that."

"So you found a look-alike, or made you one with a little help from medical science. Don't you know she was just being polite, that she really didn't expect you to come?"

That comment snapped him out of his trance and he was back to his old self. His nostrils flared like a race horse. His face got red. I saw the anger I had seen before.

He got up marched over to the red dress, and fondled it. "McKay, I thought you would appreciate this room for its historical significance if nothing else. But I can see you're an uncultured man."

"All this for a woman who wouldn't give you the time of day."

"How would you know, you redneck peckerwood. My boy understands."

"Which boy?" I asked.

"Elton Junior of course."

"What about Brandon?"

"Brandon is too much of a hothead like you, McKay."

"He tried to have me killed for your approval," I said.

"He doesn't think before he acts," Parker said.

"And you do of course," I said.

"Always." He walked over to a table, picked up a red laced bra, and sniffed it. "You can still smell the perfume." For a moment he was gone again. Suddenly his eyes flashed and he was back. "Sam, I think it's time for McKay to take a long walk on a short pier."

"That's almost poetic," I said. "Did you just make that up? You have any more?"

"A wiseass to the very end, huh McKay?" he said.

Sam reached in his shirt pocket, took a cigarette from the pack and stuck it in his mouth, but didn't light it. "Time for me to earn my money, Clark. This time you don't have Pepper to save your ass."

"Just for curiosity's sake," I said, "that was you last night, wasn't it Sam?"

"You know I could have killed you if I wanted to," he said. "Brandon tried, but he's not as good a shot as I am. I was hoping you would finally give it up. I didn't want to kill you but I didn't really think you would, that's why I told the old man to look for you."

"What about Coleman?" I asked.

"Fish bait," he said. "You fucked up my plan. I told Parker he was going to the FBI."

"Cleaver in on this?"

"He didn't have a clue what was going on. I told him to guard you with his life. He did."

"What I figured. Your name should be Pinocchio."

"Does it really matter now?" Sam asked.

"I guess not," I said. "You didn't light your cigarette, Sam. You trying to quit?"

"Parker don't like the smoke."

"I don't either but it never stopped you."

"I'm not on your payroll." He rolled the cigarette around in his mouth, sucking on it like a pacifier.

"I'm sorry about Mary and your boy," Sam said. "I had a big-time crush on her. I even had wet dreams about her."

"She never did trust you."

"That hurts." Sam took his unlit cigarette from his mouth and dropped it in his shirt pocket.

"Let's go," he said. "The war is finally over and you lost." He waved his pistol at me and pointed toward the door.

The door swung open and Pepper was standing there with her .38 in one hand and the Beretta in the other.

279

"What the hell? You again!" Sam said, staring at Pepper in disbelief.

For a split second he was distracted. I grabbed his gun arm with both hands and bent it back until I heard the bone crack. He gritted his teeth, let out a loud squeal and made a monster face.

The weapon tumbled out of his hand and I caught it before it hit the floor. I kicked him in the gut and he staggered back against the wall, pulling down several Marilyn Monroe posters.

Parker lunged at Pepper. She side-stepped him, he shoved her down, grabbing at the .38 as she fell. He missed and hurriedly limped out of the room. Pepper got to her feet and took off after him.

Sam grabbed the gun in his leg holster. Before he could fire I jerked the Glock up and put two holes in his left shirt pocket, right through his pack of Marlboros. Two little red circles quickly appeared on his pocket and grew bigger every second. He grimaced and tried to pull the trigger. His hand was past working. He dropped the gun and sat down hard on the floor like he was expecting a chair to be there.

"Damn you," he said. "You always was a lucky sonofabitch."

He fell over sideways against the wall; his head resting on his shoulder, his eyes open in a dead stare.

I took off out the door in the direction Parker and Pepper had gone. Parker had slipped up behind Pepper and was reaching behind a row of books on a book shelf.

I raised the Glock toward Parker. "Move away Parker. You're dead if you don't."

Pepper wheeled around ready to fire. Parker dropped his hand from the shelf and moved away from the book case.

"I got him," I said. "Go check outside and see if we have company."

Pepper nodded, stuck her weapons in her waistband and hurried out the door.

I reached in behind the books and found an old Army .45. It was loaded.

"Well, looks like you have the upper hand," he said. "What now?"

"I don't know. I haven't made up my mind yet." I stuck Sam's gun in my belt, jerked the slide back on the .45 throwing a round in the chamber, and pushed the safety off.

Parker stood there eyeing the .45. "You're not going to shoot me, McKay, it's against your code to shoot an unarmed man," he said.

"Things change," I said.

"I paid the bastard off, but instead of giving me the file he was going to double-cross me and turn it over to the FBI," he said. "I couldn't let that happen. Take the five million and let's call it a draw. I'll even forgive you for what you did to DeAngelo and Brandon."

"The last thing I want is your forgiveness," I said.

"I'm home scot-free anyway," he said. "No evidence no case. The police are happy with who they got for the murders and the file is a memory. I had the rest of the files destroyed and there's no microfilm that anyone knows of."

"I wouldn't be too sure," I said. "You and your cohorts are responsible for thousands that didn't have to die, and maybe even a president. I can't let you get away with that."

A slight grin appeared on his face. The comment made him happy with himself. "McKay, all I'll say to that is, the easiest people to manipulate are the simple-minded with illusions of grandeur."

"The more I think about it," I said, "the more I believe no court would convict you, even with that file. You have too many people in your pocket. Maybe some of the others, but not you."

"That's what I've been trying to tell you. You're wasting your time, McKay. I'm the most powerful man in this country."

"I believe that," I said. "Do you shoot with your left hand or your right?"

"What are you talking about?"

"Do you shoot with your left hand or your right? Simple question."

"The right. What the hell does that have to do with anything?"

I took two quick steps to Parker, grabbed his arm and spun him a half turn, slammed him down in his chair, pressed the .45 to his head and blasted a bullet into his brain before he knew what was happening.

Blood, bone and gray matter flew out the other side of his head and splattered across his big beautiful mahogany desk. He had a surprised, wide-eyed expression frozen on his face, his mouth open.

I wiped the .45 clean with my shirttail, placed it in his right hand and closed his fingers around the handle.

"See you in hell, Parker. Too bad it took so long. That's one slow bullet."

Pepper came charging in the room. "I heard a shot!"

"Parker decided to do the right thing and blow his brains out…anyone out there?"

"No," she said, walking closer to Parker. "You really expect me to believe he killed himself?"

"What's it look like?"

"Looks like you blew his shit away and tried to make it look like he did it. That's what it looks like."

"Does, doesn't it? Maybe we better get out of here before someone else comes to the same conclusion. I thought I told you to stay clear of this."

"Would you rather be dead," she said.

"Yeah, I think I'll resend that order. How did you get here so fast? You were supposed to be picking up Sandy."

"I got Goodnight's wife to do it and high-tailed it up here right after I talked to you. Picked up a rental at the airport, figured I could be of more use here."

"You figured right if no one checks on you. Where's Matt?"

"He's in Turkey on assignment," she said.

"Take off, I'll meet you at the Long Shore Airport to drop off the rental," I said.

"Hurry," she said and charged out of the room.

I noticed an envelope with bloodspots on it, lying on the desk. It had International Bank of Switzerland printed on it, addressed to Elton Parker. I picked it up and opened it.

A letter inside said my authorization for the money had been approved and they could no longer prevent me from obtaining the money, unless he could get a court order stating the documents were fake. I stuck the letter back in the envelope and put it in my pocket.

I took a quick look at Sam in the Marilyn room. His unlit cigarette had fallen out of his shirt pocket when he hit the floor and was stuck in his blood. I wiped my prints off his gun and tossed it in the room. "Sorry Sam, but you had it coming."

Pepper ran back to check on me. "I'm waiting on you. Let's go before somebody shows up."

"I'm right behind you." I picked up the .357 and hurried outside.

Pepper sped away with me and the Super Sport right behind her. No one showed as we left the farm. We dropped off the rental and I let the hammer down on the Super Sport, headed for DC.

On the way back to DC I began to think about the consequences of what I did.

We got away clean but I knew it wouldn't last long. I had to get Pepper safe and try to divert any harm coming to her. Parker deserved to die but it may have cost too much. The sooner I got out of town the better for all concerned.

50

I dropped Pepper off at her house in the wee hours of the morning and managed to get a couple hours of sleep. I called to check on her later the next morning.

"You all right?" I asked.

"And you?" she said.

"I'm okay. You always show up like the cavalry to save my butt. Maybe you were right. Time for me to ride off into the sunset and let you younger ones take care of the bad guys."

"I'll take you for a partner anytime," she said.

"Thanks Pepper. Watch your back. There's going to be some unhappy people in this town soon."

"That would make my dad happy"

"Yeah I think so. It may be to your advantage to take a long vacation some place that doesn't have extradition."

"Might be time to see how good of a lawyer I am," she said.

"Let me know if you need me."

"I'll do that."

"One last thing," I said, "you should marry that boy."

"I think I will. You take care of yourself. I'm only a phone call away."

"What do you want me to do with the money in Switzerland?"

"I don't want it. I got a large settlement from mom and dad's insurance. Bobby had an insurance policy for a million made out to me and Aunt Sara. I don't need it, and I would feel guilty about it anyway. Keep it or do whatever you want with it."

"I don't want it either, but I think I know a good place for it."

"Do it," she said.

"Okay. Billie has asked me to come to Paris for a while. It might be good to get out of Dodge."

"Parker committing suicide like that was a surprise," she said.

"Like Goodnight once told me, you never know what people will do," I said.

"That's for sure. Let me know when the wedding is."

"Got to. You have to give me away."

"Anytime, see you Amanda."

"Bye. I love you," she said.

"I love you too," I said and hung up.

I stood on the bank of the Potomac under a cherry blossom tree, looking at the blue steel revolver in my hand. We had been through a lot together, but my job was done; it was time to move on. I tossed it in the river, thanked Cleaver for it and walked away.

I swung by the kennel and picked up Scooter. He was a lot friendlier this time. Mr. Morgan said animals can sense things, maybe they can. I was all he had and he knew t. He licked my hand and we went for a hamburger. We both eat every bite of our burgers.

It was five thirty in the afternoon when I got to Goodnight's. I rang the doorbell and Julie came to the door.

"Clark, we were worried about you. Come in, Sonny's in the den," she said and retreated to the kitchen.

Sonny was stretched out on the couch with his bad leg propped up on a pillow, watching TV. Mary Ann and one of the boys were playing with some building blocks.

"Clark," Sonny said. "Glad to see you back."

"Thanks," I said.

Mary Ann ran over to me. "Mommy's in the kitchen."

"Thank you, sweetheart." She took my hand and led me into the kitchen.

"You made it back," Sandy said and smiled.

"Yeah, I think it's over now. You can go home."

"That's good." She didn't sound too happy about it.

"I have a dog in the car, so I can't stay long."

"Where did you get a dog?" she asked, surprised.

"He's been in a kennel. He belonged to a friend of mine that's dead now. I kind of inherited him."

"What are you going to do with him?"

"Keep him, I guess. He didn't like me very much, but we made up."

"I'll walk out with you," she said.

"I got to go, Sonny, I'll see you tomorrow."

"Stick around and we'll watch some games or something," he said.

"Maybe tomorrow."

"Anytime, I'm not going anywhere."

"See everybody tomorrow," I said and waved. They waved back. Sandy walked outside with me.

"Clark, I forgot to thank you for the tires," she said. "When I asked where they came from they said a tall man with blue eyes and a southern drawl as thick as molasses paid cash for them. I knew that had to be you."

"It was my fault. I owed you."

"I know you got to go. You can tell me what happened in Long Shore tomorrow."

"Yeah, tomorrow is better."

When I got back in the car Scooter was curled up on the back seat, asleep. That seemed like a good idea. I needed some rest.

After a stop at McDonalds for a burger for both of us, I found a motel and we settled in for the night.

To my surprise, I had become very fond of Scooter in such a short period of time; and I think he had of me, too.

Maybe he knew we needed each other.

51

The next morning I woke early after a restless night, made a pot of coffee, got Scooter a candy bar from the vending machine, and we watched the morning news lying in bed.

A news bulletin came on:

"State Department diplomat and entrepreneur Elton S. Parker and FBI Agent Samuel Glenn Tuit were found dead this morning at Mr. Parker's dairy farm in Long Shore, New York by Mr. Parker's Butler. Authorities said it appeared that Mr. Parker's death was a self-inflicted gunshot to the head. FBI Agent Sam Tuit's death is being investigated. It is not clear yet why Agent Tuit was at the farm."

"Hey Scooter, you see that? Poor man killed himself. I never knew what the 'S' stood for." Scooter twisted his head and went back to working on the last piece of the Snickers bar.

I drank the rest of my coffee then called Sandy and asked if she and Mary Ann would like to have breakfast with me and Scooter. She said yes. I told her I would pick them up in an hour.

We went to a nearby restaurant. The lady at the front said I couldn't bring the dog inside.

"He don't come in, we don't come in," I said.

"Well alright," she said, "but you're responsible for his behavior."

"Fair enough." I put Scooter under my arm and we found a booth and sat down. I sat Scooter next to me and tied a napkin around his neck. A pretty young lady came over to take our order, looked at Scooter, laughed and patted him on the head.

"He's a good tipper," I said, trying to add a bit of levity.

She laughed again and took the order. We ordered breakfast and I got Scooter his favorite, a big hamburger with just meat and cheese. Mary Ann fed it to him, and he showed his gratitude by licking her hand between bites.

"I saw the news this morning," Sandy said. "I was shocked. I couldn't believe Parker killed himself."

"You're probably not the only one," I said.

"What about Brandon?"

"I think he's learned his lesson. He could have a murder charge hanging over him without daddy to protect him. I think he will take off. If he doesn't, Elton Junior will run him off. If by some chance I'm wrong, you call me. I promise he won't bother you again."

"What are you going to do now, Clark?"

"I'm going to go to Paris, France for a while. My sister-in-law invited me to spend some time getting reacquainted. I think I will, let things cool off. After that, I don't know"

"Sonny told me about your family and friends. I'm very sorry," she said, placing her hand on mine, touching what was left of my little finger. "Sorry, he told me about that too."

"Methinks Sonny talks too much."

"He was just concerned about you. He said he never met a man with more intestinal fortitude."

"Oh he did, did he?"

"Well, I dressed it up a bit. What he actually said was guts," she said and smiled.

"He's not bad himself," I said.

"Why don't you come back to Long Shore with me and Mary Ann?"

"Thank you, but I have to find out who I am again, Sandy. That will take a while."

"You're always welcome," she said.

"That means a lot. Thank you, from the bottom of my heart."

Later that day I put Sandy and Mary Ann on a flight home. I booked me a flight to Paris, called and told Billie, to her surprise, to pick up Scooter at the airport...he was on his way to Paris.

As I was walking through the airport parking lot to my car two men approached me, both casually dressed wearing jackets and open-collar shirts. One was a little younger than me, redheaded, average build. The other one younger than the redhead, trimmer, maybe Hispanic, wearing dark sun shades.

"Mister McKay?" The older one asked.

I hesitated for a moment and checked my avenues of escape. "Yes," I said, keeping my distance.

"We're from the CIA." They stopped a few feet from me and showed me badges that looked like the real thing. "I'm

Agent Carter," the older one said, "and this is Agent Martinez." Martinez nodded.

"And..?" I said, waiting for a comment.

"Could we see some I.D. just to confirm things?" Carter asked.

I took my wallet out of my pocket and showed him my driver's license.

"That your current address?" Carter said, looking at the license.

"Officially it is. Don't stay at the house much anymore, kind of move around."

"Thank you." Carter handed the license back to me. "We checked the ticket counter and see you're going to Paris. We think that's a good idea," he said. "You should consider staying there indefinitely. We don't have enough evidence to detain you, but we know you had something to do with Elton Parker's death and Agent Tuit. Just not enough to arrest you yet."

"Sounds like you been talking to Junior," I said.

"If you mean Senator Elton Parker Junior, we have," Carter said. "He seems to think you have a vendetta against his family and doesn't understand why."

"You people never cease to amaze me with your arrogance."

"Mr. McKay," Martinez said, "we're trying to give you the benefit of the doubt at this time. You should take it."

"And if I don't?"

"Then we will have to deal with you as we see fit," Martinez said. "There's good reason for what we do. We have to protect this country in whatever way is necessary. We can't let you expose our work."

"Or your illegal activities," I said.

"You're not listening, Mr. McKay." Martinez took off his shades and gave me a hard stare from his dark brown eyes. "Forget what you learned from the file."

"If I'm not under arrest I'll go now."

"You're free to go, for now," Carter said. "Take some good advice and stay in Paris."

Martinez nodded his head in agreement as they walked away.

This was Monday. The mail should be arriving at its destination from the weekend today or tomorrow. We'll see if anyone else will do what is necessary for the good of the county.

52

I drove back to Goodnight's. He was sitting in a swing on the front porch with a blanket laying across his legs. He looked bored.

"Penny for your thoughts," I said as I stepped up on the porch.

"I saw the news on Parker and Sam this morning," he said. "It's kind of disturbing, I asked Baldona to check into it for me. He said they may be changing the Parker suicide to a homicide. And if it was a homicide they think the same person killed Sam.

"Parker's butler said a man came to Parker's mansion and they had a disagreement, but he didn't catch his name. The description he gave sounded a lot like you. They're going to talk to his sons. I don't know if you had anything to do with it for sure and I don't want to know. I do think you're doing the right thing by getting out of the country for a while."

"You're not the only one." I said.

"Yeah, we'll leave it at that," he said.

"Good. How you feeling?"

"Frustrated as a woodpecker in a petrified forest. I'll be glad when I can get back to work. By the way, thanks for watching out for my family while I was laid up."

"He must have thought better of it," I said.

"Yeah, something like that. You get Sandy and Mary Ann off okay?" he asked, repositioning his bad leg on the swing.

"Yeah, they're on their way home."

"She's a good woman. You should plan on seeing her again."

"I'm old enough to be her father."

"Well you're not."

"True," I said.

"Julie and I enjoyed having them. We made a new friend. I know the boys did."

"I have a noon flight," I said.

"I thought if you could get that bum leg of yours in the car you could drive me to the airport, give you something to do."

"I think I can do that. I don't need my left leg to drive, just dance." He thought he made a funny and laughed.

"You got a dollar?" I asked, cutting off his laugh.

"What do you need a dollar for?"

"To finish a little business deal. Give me a dollar."

"Here," he said, pulling a dollar out of his wallet with a puzzled look.

"Thanks. You just bought a Seventy-Three Chevy Super Sport." I handed him the keys and title.

"I can't take your car," he said, trying to give the title and keys back to me.

"It's not my car. I sold it to you. A deal's a deal."

"Julie come out here!" he yelled. "Clark has lost his mind!"

Julie came to the door. "What's all this yelling about?"

"Clark sold me his car for a dollar and won't take it back."

"Oh don't be silly." She gave a hand wave and walked back in the house.

"I mean it. I can't take it to Paris with me. I don't know how long I'll be gone. Now drive me to the airport in your new car."

He hobbled to the car and we drove away. When we pulled up to the airport entrance he cut the engine off and looked at me.

"Clark, we may never see each other again. I wanted you to know I count you as a true friend. They picked up the guy that was snooping around my house for burglary in Maryland, and he told them about you and wanted to file charges for attempted murder for playing Russian Roulette with him. They called me. I would have never known. Thank you for protecting my family."

"I appreciate all you did for me and the Spiciers, too,' I said.

"You earned it."

"You ever find who did Overa? I would like to shake his hand."

"No, but when we do I'll let you know."

"Good. Thanks for the ride."

"I don't think it's over," he said. "They will come for you, either the law or the Parkers. Never let you guard down."

"I did what I had to do."

"I'm sure you think you did but sometimes the price is too high."

"Not this time."

"Good luck. And goodbye," he said.

"Goodbye," I said. We shook hands. I opened the door and stepped out with my bag, closed the door and waved as he drove away.

I felt like a weight had been taken off my shoulders. I made it right for Robert and his family, and finally got myself together. I knew that would please Mary and Cooper, and the guys on the wall could rest a little better now.

53

On my flight to Paris I watched *The Godfather* and dozed. It was the first time I felt relaxed in a long time. The need for whisky was becoming less of a problem for me, but I knew the only way to keep it that way was to never have another drink for the rest of my life.

Billie picked me up and we had dinner at one of the sidewalk cafés and reminisced about Mary and Cooper. She drank wine and I drank tea. It was the first time I had been able to talk about them in five years.

The next morning Scooter and I took a run to McDonalds. A Big Mac is a Big Mac no matter where you are.

When we came back, Billie had left a note saying she had to go out and would be back in two or three hours.

I tried to watch TV but there wasn't enough English programming and my French was very limited.

My cell phone rang. It was Nina from Switzerland.

"Mr. McKay, I checked like you asked me. The money in Mr. Spicier's account has been cleared. We have your power of attorney on file. You can leave it here or have it transferred to any account you choose."

"Thank you." I hung up and called Sandy.

"Clark, I didn't expect to hear from you so soon," she said.

"I didn't expect to call so soon. I want to send Mary Ann a little money for her birthday."

"Her birthday is four months away."

"Alright, then this is a pre-birthday gift. You see that she spends it wisely."

"Sure, if that's what you want to do."

"That's what I want to do. What's your account number?"

"I don't mind giving you the account number, but why don't you mail it?"

"I'm afraid it might get lost."

She gave me the account number and I had five million wired to Sandy Wiggins 1st National Bank Long Shore New York, transaction complete. Parker's orphan blood-money had found a good home.

Scooter jumped up in my lap. We had become quick buddies.

Thunder cracked and I saw lightning streak across the sky. By the time the sound faded it started to rain.

This was a good time for me and Scooter to take a nap. I laid down on the couch and Scooter stretched out on the white shaggy rug. I fell into a deep peaceful sleep for the first time in years.

Later I woke up having trouble breathing. My eyes were watering and the room was spinning. I called Scooter but he didn't move.

Through the swirling blackness it came to me...

Trilene.

"Junior, you sonofabitch."

AFTERWORD

The traumatic effect of war on a combat soldier is documented throughout history. Once thrown into the horror of battle a combat soldier's life is changed forever, just as the life of Clark McKay in this novel.

A soldier may not have nightmares but he will never be the same again. Innocence is lost and the realization of the cruelty of man becomes shockingly clear.

No soldier should have to go into combat without the assurance he was sent to win and with all the resources his country possesses available to him – to not only win a battle, but to win a war.

And now a special excerpt from
John L. Lansdale's next novel:

Horse of a Different Color

Available August 2017
in Hardcover and Digital formats
from BookVoice Publishing

Horse of a Different Color

John L. Lansdale

BookVoice Publishing 2017

PROLOGUE
OFFICER DOWN

WARD FIVE, HOUSTON, TEXAS
12:05 A.M.
THE PROJECTS

She lay on the bare mattress, naked, in a spread-eagle position on her back; her beautiful body drenched in sweat and her wet green eyes wide with fear. Her mouth was covered with duct tape and her hands and feet bound to the bed post with leather straps. A foul smell of dampness and decay filled the empty room.

Rain drops tapped on the dirty windows and the car lights made the rain drops look like sparkling rhinestones as they slid down the windows in the wee hours of the night.

A door opened and a tall, wet shadow appeared in the open doorway. She could make out the vague image of a gun. Tears ran down her cheeks; she fought at the straps.

She screamed but no sound came out. The shadow stepped inside the door and shined a flashlight on her.

"It's alright, I'm a cop," he said.

She closed her eyes and sighed. They found her. She had been rescued. Her prayers were answered.

Suddenly, a second shadow appeared in the doorway behind the first, holding something long and shiny. She squirmed and darted her eyes back and forth, shook her head up and down as a warning, but the dark night betrayed her and the cop kept moving toward her.

Then she saw it. It was a knife, a killing knife, in the hand of the dark figure behind the cop. In the blink of an eye, the knife plunged into his body. Blood gushed out and ran down his back. He crumbled to the floor, his gun sliding from his hand.

HOUSTON MEMORIAL HOSPITAL
ONE MONTH LATER

In room 649 of the physical rehabilitation ward, Rustin Kemp struggled to raise his thirty-year-old, six-foot-three body up in bed on the pull-up bar. His blue eyes showed the pain as he tugged on the bar.

Sunlight splashed across the walls of the room through a window on a bright autumn day, painting them with a multi-colored pattern. A red porcelain vase with a dozen red roses in it and a card propped against it read, "Get well soon - from all the gang."

Rustin's boss, Captain Bill Lucas, stood beside the bed, his thin brown hair showing a shiny bald spot. Sagging jaws rested on the collar of a white shirt under a dark blue suit coat and a red tie draped over a pudgy belly swung back and forth like a pendulum.

"Everyone wanted to let you know they were thinking of you," he said. "Thought I would deliver the flowers and see how you were doing. The son of a bitch left you for dead."

Rustin dropped his hands from the pull bar, adjusted his pillow and looked at Bill Lucas.

"Can't walk yet," he said, "but the Doc thinks I will. I won't be doing any dancing, but I may be able to get around good enough to find that bastard if it's the last thing I ever do."

"I hope so, Rustin, but as my daddy used to say on the farm, 'We got a hard row to hoe.' No DNA, nothing except the horrific things he did to her. Homicide has had a crew on the case ever since you went down. It looks like she partied too hard and ran into the wrong guy. He may be in jail for something else, or laying low for a while."

"He'll show up," Rustin said. "The sick ones always do. I have to get out of this bed. There's something in the back of my mind that keeps bugging me. Something I need to remember that won't come to me."

"Rustin, if you hadn't been chasing that crackhead and stumbled in on her she may have disappeared like a lot of the others, and then no one would have known what happened to her. Unfortunately, it didn't turn out good. But at least her family got to bury her."

"All the more reason I have to find him, Bill."

"What you need to do is concentrate on getting well."

"I am, and I'll be planning how I'm going to catch that son of a bitch, too."

"You're a hard-headed man, Rustin."

"Been told that before."

Bill laughed and patted Rustin on the arm.

"Oh, I'm going to walk again. You can count on that."

"If you need anything let me know."

"I will. Tell everyone at the station I said thanks."

1

ONE YEAR LATER

Julie Crawford just turned twenty-one. She was celebrating her adulthood on a Saturday night in downtown Warfield, Texas with friends and some of the club regulars at Griffin's Bar and Grill. Griffin's looked like a bastard cousin to Applebee's, with a smaller menu and a longer bar.

"Hey everybody," Julie said, standing up. "This is my last night at Griffin's. My grandpa left me a bundle; I'm headed to Hollywood to be an actress! I don't have to worry about going to law school anymore to please mommy and daddy."

A tall, thin, elderly gentleman in the back of the room with white hair to his shoulders stood up holding a glass of beer. "I propose a toast to the birthday girl," he said. "She's certainly pretty enough to be a movie star. I'm old enough to remember June Allison. Julie reminds me of her, and the world could use another June Allison."

Everyone stood up, raised their glasses, gave a cheer and drank.

"Thanks everybody!" Julie said. "That's Mr. Rod Burger, my private drama coach who proposed the toast. He's a little prejudiced since my folks pay him a small fortune to train me."

Everyone laughed.

About midnight, Julie went to pee and never came back.

Two days later, two guys fishing found her mutilated body floating in the Trinity River. The police report said it would be a week before the cause of death could be determined.

At the request of the Warfield Police Department, Dallas PD sent fifteen-year veteran Detective Thomas Mecana to investigate.

Mecana was a tall, square-jawed, good-looking poster-type ex-Marine with brown wavy hair and penetrating gray eyes. He prided himself on staying fit and looked ten years younger than his forty-two-year-old body: A complete opposite to the Police Chief of Warfield, who looked like an eggplant.

Mecana's wife divorced him and moved to Austin ten years ago with his two daughters. For caring more about his job than his family, she claimed.

After researching a variety of recent murders, Mecana discovered that a murder in Houston had something in common with Julie. The vagina had been removed from both victims. Could be this sicko had come to Warfield, Mecana thought, and there would be more murders. Most of the information Mecana passed on to the Warfield Police was wasted. They wanted it all to go away and to get back to writing speeding tickets and working security for private businesses for extra money.

Warfield Police Chief David Orr was working on his second McDonalds Super Breakfast when the telephone rang.

"Warfield Police, Chief Orr speaking."

"Chief, my name's Rustin Kemp. I was involved in the Belmont murder case here in Houston last year. The Crawford murder sounds like the same MO."

"Yeah, you're not the only one. We got a detective here on the Crawford case that thinks it might be the same guy. I remember reading about you last year," Orr said. "He stabbed you and got away." Orr stuck a fork in a piece of sausage and jammed it in his mouth. "You still on the Houston force?"

"Doing private eye work now. I want that son of a bitch bad. I wanted to come up and take a look."

"Don't have a problem with that. I'll take all the help I can get, but you'll have to clear it with Detective Tom Mecana in Dallas. He's the lead guy on the case."

"I've heard of him. I'll call him, Chief. Thanks."

"No problem," Orr said, and went back to eating his breakfast.

2

Rustin looked up from his pancakes and saw Bill Lucas coming toward him. He wondered why Bill was at IHOP, he usually ate breakfast at home. He would always say, with a laugh, that nobody could cook instant oatmeal better than his Amy.

"Thought I would find you here," Bill said.

Rustin removed his cane from the empty chair and offered Bill a seat.

"Man, looking at those pancakes makes me hungry." Lucas said.

"I thought Amy always fixed your breakfast."

"I cheat sometimes," Bill said and sat down.

A cute, dark-haired waitress with 'Maria' on her name tag stopped at the table, poured Bill a cup of coffee and asked if he was ready to order.

"Yes. I'll have a stack of blueberry pancakes and sausage to go with my coffee, Maria."

"That oatmeal didn't go very far, huh, Bill?"

"Don't tell Amy. She's always nagging me about my weight."

"Not a word, I promise," Rustin said, grinning.

"Good. Got a call from Tom Mecana yesterday," Lucas said and took a sip of coffee. "You know who he is?"

"Yes. He's probably solved more murder cases than anyone else in Texas."

"Right. He wanted to know why you were trying to butt in on his case. I told him you didn't work for me anymore and I didn't have a clue what he was talking about. He said he didn't need any half-ass cops. I got to thinking about it this morning, figured you would be here since Debbie decided to take a powder, and find out what the hell was going on."

"I haven't talked to him," Rustin said. "The Police Chief in Warfield must have. The case he's talking about is a lot like the Belmont one. I was going to have a look but I needed his approval. I guess that's a no."

"Get you a client. Maybe the girl's folks. He may not help you but he can't stop you from earning a living."

"True. That would give me the right to be there," Rustin said, and took the last bite of his pancakes and reached for his wallet.

The waitress brought Bill his breakfast and poured him a fresh cup of coffee. He wolfed the pancakes down, pushed the empty plate away and picked up his coffee cup.

"Heard anything from Debbie?" he asked, and blew on the coffee.

"Nope, she said she needed to get away for a while to think things over. That was last Friday, haven't heard a word from her since. Her sister called for her, said she was at her folks'. Knew I would be worried. What she couldn't handle was me being a cripple."

"Well if that's her reason you're probably better off with out her. Think she would have done the same thing if you had been wounded in Iraq?"

"Don't know. Got out of there without a scratch and then this happens. You never know what cards you're going to be dealt."

"Good thing you don't have any kids to worry about."

"We tried. After three miscarriages we gave up."

"You should have called for backup that night. Maybe things would be different. You wouldn't be in this shape."

"Like they say, hindsight is 20/20. I thought I could handle it."

"Sounds like he's back in business," Bill said, holding his empty cup up for Maria to see.

"Don't know for sure what I'm going to do. Everything seems to get more complicated every day."

"Only you can decide that, partner. But it should be over for you. Let it go before you wind up getting hurt, physically and mentally."

"I know you mean well, Bill, but it's easier said than done. It won't let me go. It's chewing my insides up." The waitress passed by with the coffee pot, looked at Bill and poured him another cup. "I'll let you know what I decide to do, Bill, thanks."

Rustin picked up his cane and stood up. "My treat," he said, and dropped a twenty on the table.

"Thanks. Take care," Lucas said.

Rustin nodded and limped away.

3

Rustin arrived at the rehab center ten minutes before his appointment, took a couple of pain pills and made a call to Debbie's parents in Beaumont. They said she was there but didn't want to talk to him. She was going to file for divorce and her lawyer would be in touch. That was that.

The therapy lasted an extra hour because the doctor said he was not making enough progress with his weight lifts. He needed to strengthen his leg muscles more to compensate for the nerve damage in his back. Debbie would have agreed with that. When they had sex she had to do all the work. That wouldn't be a problem anymore.

Eight years down the drain. He thought about driving to Beaumont and begging her to come back, but it would probably be a waste of time and he wasn't sure his pride would let him do it any way.

He did ten more lifts with the leg weights, pulled himself up to a sitting position, picked up his cane, placed both hands on it and lifted himself up, leaning on the cane. The right leg was the one he supported most of his weight on, and the left with the cane. The pain got really bad sometimes; he needed his pills to keep going.

His doctor quit writing prescriptions for fear of him becoming addicted and told him to get some over-the-counter pain medicine if he needed it. That was a moot point now. With a new doctor in Dallas he should be able to get what he needed, at least for a while.

He reached in his pocket, got his phone and dialed.

He heard a voice say, "Lucas here."

"Bill, I decided to go to Dallas to find that prick. I wanted to say goodbye and thank you for everything."

"I understand where you're coming from, son, but don't you think you should quit while you're ahead and just move on? You're working with a big disadvantage."

"That has occurred to me but I don't have much of a life at the moment anyway, and those young women he mutilated never had a chance at any kind of life. A leopard can't change his spots. It has to be him. He leaves a gruesome calling card."

"That he does. Keep in touch."

"I will. See you."

Rustin limped to his Ford Explorer and drove home to an empty house. Everywhere he looked he saw reminders of Debbie. She was his high school sweetheart. He was the quarterback and she was a pretty blonde-haired, blue-eyed cheerleader. They had big dreams for their future. Everyone said they looked like the perfect couple.

He dropped his cane to the floor, sat down on the bed and tears came rolling down his cheeks. The only reason he had for living was to catch that bastard.

He wiped the tears away, packed a suitcase and decided he would wait until he got to Dallas to call his mom and dad to watch the house. He locked the front door, put the key in the mailbox, put his suitcase in the Explorer and headed up Interstate 45 to Dallas, into a setting sun and the unknown.

About the Author

John L. Lansdale was born and raised in East Texas. He is married to the love of his life Mary. They have four children. He is a retired Army Reserve Psychological Operations Officer and a combat veteran with numerous medals and awards. He's an inventor, country music songwriter, performer and television programmer.

He produced and directed the Television Special "Ladies of Country Music." He has produced several albums in Nashville, hosted his own radio shows and won awards for producing and writing radio and TV commercials. He was a writer and editor of a business newspaper.

He has worked as a comic book writer for Tales from the Crypt, IDW, Grave Tales, Cemetery Dance and several more. He co-authored the Shadows West and Hell's Bounty novels with his brother Joe R. Lansdale.

He has also authored the following novels in the process of publication: Zombie Gold, Slow Bullet, Horse of a Different Color, Long Walk Home, The Last Good Day, When the Night Bird Sings, and several more.

Titles available by
John L. Lansdale

Slow Bullet
Zombie Gold
Hell's Bounty (with Joe R. Lansdale)
Shadows West (with Joe R. Lansdale)
Yours Truly, Jack the Ripper (Comic Series)
Tales from the Crypt (Comic Series)

Coming Soon

Horse of a Different Color (first time in print)
Long Walk Home
The Last Good Day
Broken Moon
When the Night Bird Sings (Novella)
Shadow Warrior (Graphic Novel)
Justin Case (Graphic Novel)

What others are saying about John L. Lansdale

"*Zombie Gold* has something for everyone…
It's exciting, entertaining and educational.
A fun ride."
– Joan Hallmark, legendary TV personality, actress and author

"…something unique and comfortable and
difficult to put down. Highly recommended."
– Blu Gilliand, 'Cemetery Dance' review of *Hell's Bounty*

"True to Lansdale tradition, John L. Lansdale
has compiled a piece of work that should
appeal to a wide range of readers."
– Ricky L. Brown, 'Amazing Stories' review of *Zombie Gold*

HORSE OF A DIFFERENT COLOR
by John L. Lansdale

Available August 2017 from BookVoice Publishing

Someone is murdering and mutilating young women in a Dallas suburb, using the same techniques as a case down in Houston from a year ago.

When the second body is found, it seems the killer has moved his hunting grounds to the Dallas area.

As the body count rises, Detective Thomas Mecana – a divorced fifteen-year veteran of the Dallas Police Department – is assigned to the case.

He prides himself on always getting his man, but his tried-and-true methods of the past are not working.

To make matters worse, his supervisor assigns him a new partner - a beautiful female officer who has never before worked a murder case.

Add in two teenage daughters creating problems at home, and a boss threatening to fire him at work, and Mecana's life begins to unravel as he hones in on his suspect.

With hard work, and some luck, Mecana and his partner discover a most-unusual serial killer case with **murder** *in its very genes.*

They discover some evidence is so strange and unbelievable, it might be best left alone.

Checkmate.

Keep your eyes peeled for

The Last Good Day
by John L. Lansdale

A Weird Western

Coming Soon in 2017 from BookVoice Publishing

Watch for updates on author news, book release dates, signing locations and much more!

www.facebook.com/johnllansdale
www.twitter.com/johnllansdale
www.goodreads.com/johnllansdale

Follow **BookVoice Publishing** online at
www.bookvoicepublishing.com

CPSIA information can be obtained
at www.ICGtesting.com
Printed in the USA
LVOW12*1509280118
564331LV00005B/31/P

9 780999 036112